I0549537

TOXIC TECH

SAM CHEEVER

ELECTRIC PROSE PUBLICATIONS

PRAISE FOR SAM CHEEVER

Sam Cheever creates some of the best characters you could ever find in the pages of a book.
SensualReads.com

Ms. Cheever writes with class, humor and lots of fun while weaving an excellent story.
The Romance Studio

~

A dead vet tech...an activist group bent on destruction... and an adorable little dog that proves moxie has nothing at all to do with size.

For Blaise Runa, a job working the front desk at the local veterinary clinic is a fun but temporary diversion...a chance to spend every day with Miss Ivy, her adorable fur baby, while she continues to search for a career.

Unfortunately, the fun is soon sucked right out of the job when Blaise discovers one of the veterinary technicians poisoned in the kennel. The attack is quickly labeled the work of an activist group that resents the medical and financial resources "squandered" on pets.

But is there something less obvious...and possibly more sinister...at work?

Working alone and swimming against the tide of general opinion, Blaise soon suspects that she and her yummy fiancée, Dolfe Honeybun, might be fighting for more than justice for the vet tech. They might actually be battling to save a whole clinic full of beloved pets from someone who would be happy to see them dead. And if they're not very careful, sweet little Miss Ivy might take her place at the top of a killer's list.

_T_he giant yellow snake slithered more tightly around Blaise's throat, its tongue snapping out to taste the air beside her ear.

Blaise swallowed hard and reached up to tug on the thick body, trying to gain some air.

The reptile's body shivered, easing the pressure just enough to give her hope, and then oozed back to the place where discomfort lived on the edge of fear.

Blaise gritted her teeth and fought through it, knowing that to give in to the fear was to let the snake win.

The woman standing across the desk from her was wearing golf balls for eyes behind her oversized square glasses. Blaise wasn't sure the woman had even swallowed since arriving there.

"Punkin's gonna need to come back and get those stitches checked," Blaise said in a strangled voice.

She held the receipt out to the client but the woman didn't move to take it.

The massive yellow body oozed another quarter inch tighter and Blaise had to jam a hand behind the coil at her throat, tugging a little harder to show the snake she meant business. "Ma'am?"

The woman blinked her golf balls and shook her head, turning on her heel and all but running out the front door, her fat, little pug struggling to keep up.

Blaise turned to the gangly millennial with his head in the giant terrarium. "Adam, are you about done? I think Odyssey's settling in for the kill."

He gave the inside of the tank a final swipe and straightened, eyeing the snake's habitat with a critical and, Blaise was learning, nit-picky eye. "I just need to go grab his branch. I hosed it off out back."

Blaise rolled her eyes and twitched as something crept through her peripheral vision. The snake's head hovered on the air a few inches from her face.

If she'd been squeamish it would have been very disconcerting.

She gave the snake side-eye and its tongue forked the air an inch from her cheek.

Okay, she was a tiny bit squeamish. "Adam?"

The bell on the front door jangled and a gruff, familiar male voice said, "Holy crap!"

Blaise turned to grin at her very sexy fiancée. She was slightly concerned to see that he'd turned an unattractive pale green color. "What's wrong? Is Miss Ivy okay?" Panic flared. "What's Badly gotten into now?"

The puppy in Dolfe's arms gave her a happy yip, too delighted to see her to worry about the massive reptile wound around her neck. But a high-pitched shrieking commenced from the area around Dolfe's big feet. Blaise looked down at the tiny dog bouncing on the end of a leash, her brown eyes bulging and her enormous ears twitching with alarm.

"It's okay, Miss Ivy..." she started to say.

"Don't move, Blaise!" Dolfe took an uncertain step in her direction and then stopped, looking from the snake to his hands and then to the two dogs. "I need a weapon."

Miss Ivy was becoming more alarmed by the second. She was barking in rapid-fire bursts and her voice had reached dolphin pitch. The staccato emissions were coming so hard they tugged her off the ground, until she pinged off the floor with every bark.

"Why do you need a weapon?" Blaise asked Dolfe on a frown.

He saw an umbrella stand by the door and reached for the biggest one, snatching it up and advancing toward Blaise with murder in his eye. "Don't worry, honey. I'll save you."

Despite his brave words, she took note of the way

he seemed to have to drag his big feet forward the closer he got to the snake.

Blaise opened her mouth to tell him not to worry when Ivy shot forward, her tiny body jerking in desperation against the leash.

Odyssey's big head lowered and his eyes locked on the little dog. His tongue scraped Ivy's scent from the air.

"No!" Blaise shrieked.

"Ivy!" Dolfe roared.

Odyssey's head shot downward, faster than Blaise had ever seen the big predator move.

Dolfe threw himself between the snake and the dog just as a skinny arm snagged the reptile around the body and yanked him away.

A tense pause hung on the air, and then something slammed against the glass front door and everybody jumped. Odyssey constricted with alarm, his big head swiveling toward the sound and his tongue sliding out to test the air.

"Ccchhhh," Blaise said, slipping two fingers behind the muscular body. "Ccchhh!"

Adam grabbed the snake just behind his head and tugged on his massive body with the other hand, depriving the boa of his afternoon Blaise snack just in time.

"Sorry, Blaise." Adam's lean muscles bulged as he fought to unwind the snake from Blaise's shoulders.

She sagged downward, her knees buckling at the

close call. Odyssey had been "literally" around humans all his life. He was as sensitive as a reptile could be to the rules about eating people. But Miss Ivy was barely bigger than the rat he ate for dinner the night before.

In his cold, reptilian gaze she'd be fair game.

Blaise looked up finally, realizing Dolfe hadn't spoken for a full minute. She almost cried when she saw him. He was standing there shuddering, one tiny dog tucked under each arm and his lips moving as he cooed reassuring words to Miss Ivy. The little female was trembling so hard she would have vibrated right out of his arms if he hadn't had her in a death grip.

Blaise came around the counter and wrapped her arms around all three of them, earning herself wet kisses on the cheek from Badly the puppy and a tongue in the ear from Miss Ivy. "It's okay, you guys. I'm fine."

Dolfe returned the hug, his heart pounding hard and fast under her ear. "I wish I could say the same about us. The girl and I were pretty sure you were about to become snake kibble."

Blaise cleared her throat and coughed. "You..." Her voice sounded strained so she cleared it again. "You don't really think I'd make it that easy for him, do you?" She reached out and pulled Badly from Dolfe's grip, dodging his fast-moving tongue as she laughed. "At least Badly wasn't worried."

"He's a puppy. He's happy stupid." Dolfe sighed, scrubbing a big hand over his face before handing a still-trembling Ivy to Blaise. "I just have one thing to say. This new job of yours is going to be the death of me."

Dolfe pointed to the slimy yellow mess sliding down the outer door. "How long have those protesters been out there?"

"I think since just after lunch." She peered through the door, frowning. "I'm not liking the escalation to egging. Last week it was just signs and really pathetic chanting."

"I heard that *Badgersville Veterinary Hospital* ended up with two broken windows last week," Adam said, lifting his dark brows. "Somebody decided throwing rocks was better than throwing eggs."

Dolfe's sexy, square jaw went taut. "I'll go have a word with them."

Normally Blaise would be okay with that. After all, her six-foot-five-inch, two hundred pound...all muscle...fiancée was a great deterrent for most people, but *Precious Pets* wasn't her business and she figured she should run it past the vet first. "Just let me ask Dr. Willis what she wants us to do."

Blaise lowered Miss Ivy to the ground and the little dog immediately tottered over to the aquarium to peer in at the freshly ensconced boa constrictor.

She gave him a heartfelt bark, all four tiny feet leaving the ground at the outburst.

For his part, Odyssey seemed only mildly interested in the rat-sized pooch since she was no longer within his available prey space.

"Come on, girlfriend. Dr. Willis will want to say hi before I take you home." Blaise gave the baby a kiss and handed him back to Dolfe. "You stay here and protect daddy," she told Badly, just to get a rise out of her sexy fiancée.

"I'm not his daddy," he said without much conviction. Blaise figured she was wearing him down. "I'll guard the door," Dolfe told her, giving her raised eyebrows when she turned his way.

"Don't put anybody in a chokehold," she told him.

Dolfe thought about it for a beat. "Okay, honey. I won't put anybody in a chokehold."

"Why did you capitulate so quickly?" Blaise asked with a frown.

Dolfe shrugged. "Because that still leaves me lots of options."

Doctor Amanda Willis was just leaving Exam Room four when Blaise found her. The thirty-something veterinarian was jotting notes on a file and she looked up with a smile when Ivy trotted over and gave her a hello bark.

"There's my little girl! How's my Miss Ivy today?"

Ivy hopped happily around the young vet's ankles, her massive ears vibrating with excitement.

"She's traumatized from seeing Odyssey try to make a snack out of me," Blaise said, laughing.

Amanda's face folded into a frown. "Are you okay? I told Adam to put him in an empty room while he cleaned the cage."

"All the rooms were busy. It's okay. I'm just teasing you. I really don't mind holding him. He and I have an understanding. I understand that he could snap me like a twig on a snakey whim and he understands that if he does, I'll come back to haunt him and make his life miserable."

Amanda shook her head. "You're crazy. You know that?"

"I've been told. Speaking of crazy..."

The vet's bright blue gaze narrowed. "The *Medical Restitution League*?"

Blaise nodded. "They've started throwing eggs."

Doctor Willis sighed. "Those people need to get lives."

The group had been around for years, occasionally harassing animal hospitals and veterinarians about the resources they "wasted" on animals when humans were having to go without and facing illness and death. They'd started out as kind of a hobby group, the butt of a lot of jokes. Nobody really took them seriously because they generally only showed up on weekends to shake a few signs and then headed off to whine and complain at the nearest Starbucks.

But since the change in the healthcare laws the group had gone rogue, some factions even turning to violence to make their point.

"Dolfe wanted to go out and talk to them but I told him I'd run it by you first."

"Good call. I'd rather he didn't. I'm trying not to antagonize them."

"Adam told me things got ugly at *Badgersville*."

Amanda sighed. "Yeah. That's why I'm trying to keep it light. I just don't want to give them any excuses to go nuclear on us."

"You can't appease bullies, Mandy. You know that, right?"

"I know. It's just that, being one vet short this week, and with this new canine flu virus going around...I just can't deal with one more thing."

"No let up on the flu yet, huh?"

"It's getting worse. I had to turn three more cases away today. We need to come up with a way to treat these infected dogs. It's so contagious I'm afraid to let them into the clinic."

"Why don't we turn the old grooming building into a temporary clinic? We can assign a couple of techs and maybe bring in a visiting vet to man it on a permanent basis until the crisis is over. That way there's no cross-contamination. Only dogs with flu symptoms go there."

Amanda stared at Blaise for so long Blaise was starting to think she had spinach between her teeth or a bat in the cave. She rubbed a finger under her nose. "What? Is there something in my nose?"

"You're a flippin' genius, Blaise."

She flushed with pleasure. "Oh. Thanks. What did I do?"

"Hopefully, you solved one of my biggest problems. If we assign only vet techs who don't have dogs at home we can really contain the problem. And maybe I can talk some of the other area vets into joining us, that would widen out the care and give our techs some downtime. I love it!" She gave Blaise a quick hug. "Let's brainstorm it in the morning. You have a great evening with your honey." Amanda kissed Ivy on the head and handed her back to Blaise.

"I will. Do you need me to do anything before I go?"

"No. But remember Ivy has her dental in the morning. No food or water after Midnight."

"Oh noes," Blaise told the little dog. "You're going to think you're dying right on the spot."

Amanda grinned. "She does like her vittles."

"Just like her mama." Blaise tucked the little dog under one arm. "I'll be here at seven thirty with our little patient here. Maybe we can brainstorm the flu clinic before we open the doors."

"Sounds like a plan. I'll bring the bagels. See you then."

When Blaise returned to the lobby, Alicia Prince was at the front desk. Alicia was one of Amanda's senior vet techs. She'd been with the practice since even before Amanda bought it from a retiring veterinarian.

"Hey, Alicia."

The woman glanced up, her plain face tight with stress. "Hey, Blaise. You leaving now?"

"I am. Are you going to be able to handle the desk and assist in back too?"

Alicia grimaced. "I'll be okay. I think we only have two more patients tonight." She glared through the front doors. "If they're brave enough to go through the gantlet out there."

The protestors had moved closer to the building. They were only about fifteen feet away and their shouts of "Save humans not Pets" were sounding angrier by the moment. It looked as if several more eggs had hit the glass doors since Blaise went back to talk to Amanda.

"Dolfe went outside to glare at them. Believe it or not, they were closer before." Alicia gave Blaise a smile.

"That's my honey. I'd better get out there before he picks somebody up and flings them into the poop zone."

Chuckling, Alicia said, "See you in the morning, hon."

The chanting burst over Blaise as she opened the door. A flash of sunlight flared into her eyes, making Blaise squint as Ivy started barking, her little body jumping in Blaise's arms with every heartfelt woof.

Dolfe was standing at the end of the sidewalk that led to the parking lot. He had Badly nestled protectively in his arms and was glaring at the crowd.

The little black and tan dog peered over Dolfe's arm, his ears drooping and his brown button eyes wide with alarm.

The protestors pretended to be defiant, screaming with extra enthusiasm as they stared right at Dolfe, but Blaise noticed they were keeping their distance.

One man stood apart from the others; a cell phone lifted as if he were taping the incident that was about to happen.

Dolfe turned as she came through the door. Ivy strained her leash, growling and barking at the angry mob. Dolfe nodded toward the little dog. "Pick her up, honey. And stay close."

Blaise couldn't believe the people brandishing signs would harm her little dog, but she looked into the faces of a couple and saw such hatred there she was shocked. Blaise scooped Ivy up and moved under Dolfe's arm, keeping a close eye on the crowd as he guided them toward his big, silver truck at the back of the lot.

She suddenly wished he'd parked closer to the door.

The crowd followed them in a menacing fashion as they crossed the lot. Dolfe's jaw was tense, his big body hard with anger. He was like a bottle rocket ready to fire.

Blaise hoped the stupid people behind them didn't do anything to set him off.

Even as she had the thought an egg burst on the windshield of the truck. It had whizzed past Blaise's ear, barely missing her. Dolfe stopped, his body hardening to stone. He turned without a word and handed Badly to her. "Get to the truck."

Blaise shook her head. "Let's just go, Honeybun."

"Go on. Get the dogs out of here."

She suddenly realized he was as worried for their safety as he was for hers. That convinced her to do as he asked. But she was coming back after putting them in the truck. If there was going to be a rumble she was going to stand by her man.

Not that he needed her help. But she'd be damned if she'd desert him.

The chanting suddenly stopped as Blaise plopped Badly and Ivy on the front seat. "Keep your heads down, kids."

She closed the door and turned to see what was going on.

Dolfe was walking toward the group. His arms arced away from his body with muscle that was rock hard, and big hands fisted, Dolfe was a six-foot-five-inch weapon of mass destruction, pointed right at the troublemakers.

If he was on your side, you were lucky. If he wasn't...well...he was a terrifying sight.

She was amused to see several members of the *Medical Restitution League* backtracking, their signs drooping in their hands.

But some of them didn't retreat. Of the dozen or so people, four stood their ground, their faces ugly with hate and their minds twisted with a fanatic's zeal.

One man, bigger than the rest, brandished his sign like a club and advanced on Dolfe.

Blaise started forward. The sign was made of painted lumber, screwed onto a sturdy piece of wood. If the man hit Dolfe with it, he could do some damage.

Fortunately, sirens split the tension in the lot, drawing everyone's eyes to the unmarked sedan taking the turn into the parking lot on two wheels. The ugly little car squealed to a stop several feet away from Dolfe and a tall woman with spiky light brown hair and flashing golden brown eyes stepped out.

Detective Brita Muldane yanked out her badge and stalked toward the protestors, her pretty face a cold mask. "It's time to break up the party, folks," she said in her no-nonsense cop voice. "You're done here."

"We have a right to hold a peaceful protest," the big man who'd threatened Dolfe growled out, his gaze still locked on Dolfe.

"Yeah, you do. But flinging eggs at people's businesses and vehicles isn't peaceful. Now you either need to move along, or I'll take you all in for trespassing and defacing private property."

The protestors started murmuring among themselves. And then began to break away in small groups and head toward the street where they'd left their cars.

Finally, only the belligerent man was left and he and Dolfe were still glaring at one another.

Brita pulled a pair of cuffs out of the back pocket of her jeans and jiggled them until the man with the sign turned a hate-filled gaze on her.

Finally, he gave her a mean smile. "I'll leave. But we'll be back tomorrow."

"As long as you're peaceful that will be fine," Brita told the man.

They watched him saunter slowly toward the street.

Brita shook her head. "These people need lives."

Blaise gave her friend a hug. "Thank you for coming. How'd you know we needed you?"

"Doctor Willis called me. She said they were

terrorizing you out here. It was lucky I was in the area." She arched a light-brown brow at Dolfe.

He tried to look innocent. "What? I wasn't going to do any real damage. But the guy threw an egg at my truck."

They all looked toward the gooey mess on Dolfe's windshield. Behind it, two diminutive heads kept popping up above the dash, followed by the strident barks of the two dogs.

Brita grinned. "Has Badly been through the car wash yet?"

"No. But that boy's not afraid of anything, Dolfe said almost proudly."

Blaise and Brita shared a grin.

"I don't know, he looked pretty worried about those protestors," Blaise told him.

"He has reason to be." Dolfe looked at Brita. "Some of those people aren't sane," he told her. "There's going to be real trouble if somebody doesn't get a handle on this."

She shrugged. "My hands are tied. We've been told to just contain the situation. The higher-ups are hoping it will all fizzle out."

"It's going to explode before it fizzles," Dolfe said, frowning. "Meanwhile, good people like Doc Willis will suffer because the Chief of Police wants to play politics."

"You aren't wrong." Brita cast a worried glance toward the building. "I'm going in to talk to Mandy.

I'll give her some advice. But ultimately, we're subject to the whim of the idiots with the signs."

Blaise sighed. "She's worried about antagonizing them."

"She's right to worry. I'll try to make a sweep through here several times a day. Maybe that will cool their jets a bit."

"Thanks, Brit." Blaise gave her another hug and turned to Dolfe, who was staring toward the street. The thug who'd brandished the sign at Dolfe was there, arms crossed over a barrel chest, staring at them. Blaise didn't like where that confrontation was heading. She hooked her arm through Dolfe's. "Come on, future husband. I'm thinking hamburgers and beers for dinner."

He let her pull him toward the truck. "Okay. But first, we need to take the truck through the car wash. If that egg sets up, it'll be nearly impossible to get off."

2

*B*laise yawned widely as she climbed out of the car the next morning. The parking lot was empty except for one car parked in the drive of the old house that used to be a grooming salon until the groomer gave up the lease and left to have a baby.

Ivy jumped out of the car and trotted over to the grassy area to do her business.

Watching her dog squat in the too-long grass, Blaise made a mental note to ask Amanda whose car that was. She didn't think her friend the vet could have already put things into motion over there.

Amanda had inherited the building along with the clinic and she'd always had it rented out, until recently. Blaise had been thinking about the flu clinic idea since leaving the evening before and she had some ideas for how Amanda could monetize it and take some of the sting out of providing care in a secondary location.

She grinned to herself. She was starting to sound like a business person. Hanging around Dolfe Honeybun had been good for her in more ways than one.

Personally, *and* professionally.

Ivy finished her business and started to mosey, her pointy little nose to the ground.

"Come on, girlfriend. Let's go inside."

The little dog fell in beside Blaise, stopping every few inches to sniff the ground where the protestors had been. "Yeah, I know, that's where the mean people were." Blaise bent down to pick up her dog but came up empty.

Ivy shot away from her, ears and tail quivering with excitement. Her bark was strident, more high-pitched than usual, which was a sign that something had alarmed her. Blaise looked in the direction her dog was staring and was surprised to see the car at the groomery backing out of the short drive.

She hurried after Ivy, scooping her up as she called out and waved. "Hello?"

The car accelerated so quickly its tires spun on the pavement, leaving behind skid marks. It barely slowed at the entrance, turning onto the busy road and speeding away.

Blaise frowned. "Who in the world?"

Shaking her head, she gave Ivy a squeeze. "Good girl. You're a perfect little watchdog."

Ivy wriggled happily in her arms, giving her a kiss on the end of her nose. "Let's get you inside. Maybe Doctor Willis knows who that was."

Blaise used her key to enter the building, placing Ivy on the ground as she closed the door. "Amanda?"

Blaise hadn't seen the vet's Jeep Wrangler parked outside, but Doctor Willis often parked in back of the building. She lived almost an hour away so she sometimes spent the night upstairs, in the bedroom she'd set up for just that reason. Blaise figured, since they'd planned to meet early, Mandy might have stayed in the building the night before.

She started upstairs. Ivy bounced ahead of her, happily shooting away into the darkness at the top of the stairs to explore the space.

Blaise passed through an open area with folding chairs that Mandy occasionally used to give information sessions to her clients. She walked through the conference room, which featured a long, well-worn farm table and a matching hutch that held an eclectic array of plates and mugs and a single serve coffee maker.

The door to the bedroom at the end of the building was open, and Blaise could see that the bed was messy. Someone had definitely slept there the night before. Mandy was probably out getting the bagels she'd promised Blaise. The door to the small bathroom off the conference area was open and the room was dark.

Blaise grabbed a couple of plates and settled them on the table. She made herself a cup of coffee and took a sip, closing her eyes on a wave of pleasure. "Yum."

Ivy brushed against her leg, whining softly. "What's wrong, little girl? Are you thirsty?"

She filled the dog bowl in the bathroom sink and set it on the floor for her dog. But when she went looking for her, she was gone.

"Ivy?"

A distant barking told Blaise the little dog had gone back downstairs. "Ivy! Come here."

The dog ignored her summons as she did all too often, and Blaise set her mug down with an irritated grunt, thinking of the cat food Mandy sometimes left down for the clinic's resident black cat. "You'd better not be eating Joe's cat food! You're having surgery later."

She bounded down the stairs and turned toward the noise of her dog having a meltdown. It sounded like she was in the tech area, where the vet techs tended the surgery patients and performed such routine things as nail cutting and anal sac emptying.

"You know you're not supposed to be in there, Miss Ivy." A low, dark form flashed past, brushing against Blaise's calf, and she skidded to a stop with a surprised yelp. Midnight Joe hightailed it through the door into the waiting area. The big cat was apparently not a fan of Ivy's strident form of communication.

"You're scaring Joe." Ivy's barking had gained a shrill note that made Blaise speed her steps. "What are you barking at...?"

Blaise stopped in her tracks, her eyes going wide. Ivy stood in front of a Great-Dane-sized kennel, the hair on her back standing straight up and her tail whipping the air like a blender behind her. Her tiny body was rigid with fear.

Blaise didn't blame her. She took a hesitant step forward, her gaze locked on the unmoving figure stuffed into the kennel. "Ivy, come here."

Ivy finally stopped barking and turned, giving a little whine. "Come here, girl."

With a final glance at the big kennel, Ivy trotted over to Blaise and allowed herself to be scooped up.

Blaise eyed the body in the kennel for movement, but knew in her heart there wouldn't be any. The victim's face was gray, her body rigid in an unnatural position.

Alicia Prince's death-glazed stare was focused on the door; her mouth opened slightly as if she'd died imploring someone for help.

But clearly, that help had never come.

manda Willis stood as far away from the kennel as she could get without leaving the room. The bag of bagels she'd arrived with was still clutched in her hand, the white paper so creased and wrung out Dolfe thought it would be a miracle if the bagels didn't look like pretzels.

Tears flowed in an endless stream down the young vet's pale cheeks. Her blue eyes were red-rimmed, and her slightly oversized nose was red. The woman was what Blaise would call an ugly crier.

"You haven't noticed anything off about her behavior lately," Brita asked Blaise's boss. "Has she had any altercations with anyone...complained about anybody bothering her?"

Amanda sniffed, shaking her head. "Nothing like that. She's been a little tense. Tired. But we've all been working extra hours because of the canine flu epidemic."

Brita nodded. "I've been keeping my dogs home and away from other dogs for two months. So far so good."

Amanda gave Brita a smile. "I'm relieved we haven't seen any of your furbabies here. It especially takes a toll on the youngest and oldest dogs."

Dolfe felt a pinprick of something in the center of his chest, recognizing it as alarm. Badly was only six months old and, though the little demon seemed bulletproof, he was no doubt just as susceptible to things like canine flu as any other dog.

"Your Danny's what? Close to fourteen? It's really important you keep her close until we can get a handle on this plague."

Brita nodded. Dolfe thought about Brita's elderly golden retriever. She was one of the sweetest dogs he'd ever met. In fact, he'd always thought he'd get a golden retriever someday. Danny was a big reason he felt that way.

"I'll do that." Brita gave the vet a beat to rein in the tears and then began to gently question her again. "Was Alicia still here when you left last night?"

Amanda nodded, scraping a hand under her nose. "She was just going to update a couple of patient records, and then her boyfriend was going to pick her up."

"Do you know if he ever came?"

"I don't. Sorry."

Blaise frowned. "You didn't stay here last night?"

Mandy looked shocked. "No. I went home." She shuddered. "I briefly considered staying though. What if I had?" She wrapped her arms around herself, clearly spooked.

"I don't suppose you have security cameras outside?" Dolfe asked hopefully.

Amanda glanced toward the back door which had been open when they arrived. According to

Mandy, the door had been locked when she left the night before. "No. But you can be sure *that* will be changing today. Between those terrible protestors and now this..." Amanda stopped, blinked, and turned a horrified glance to Brita. "You don't think one of those zealots killed Alicia?"

Brita lifted her hand, showing the vet the object she'd been holding down by her side.

It was a small metal tube with a white label. There was a picture of a dog on the label, and the words, *Soothe your best friend's pain.* "Do you recognize this ointment?" Brita asked.

"Yes. *Canine Soothe.* It's an antibiotic ointment for dogs." She frowned. "Where'd you get that?"

"Alicia Prince was holding it." Brita glanced toward the kennel. The morgue guys were there, and they were getting ready to extract the dead woman from the cage. "If I'm not mistaken, she'd used some of it on her arm." Brita indicated the center of her forearm. "She had a scratch there."

Amanda nodded. "We all do that." When Brita looked confused she clarified. "We use *Canine Soothe* on ourselves. It's actually a lot better than triple antibiotic ointment and considerably cheaper." She frowned. "I guess The *Medical Restitution League* might have a point on that, huh?" Amanda looked sad.

"Is this ointment available without a prescription?"

Amanda looked at Dolfe. "No. But we sell it here to our patients."

"So, you think Alicia got this tube from your medical supplies?" Brita held the bag up again.

Amanda hugged herself, smashing the long-suffering bagels beneath her arms. "You're very interested in that ointment."

"Alicia appears to have been poisoned. The area where I believe she applied the ointment is bright red and blistered, as are two of the fingers of her right hand. I think the salve might have been doctored with something."

Amanda's hand flew to cover her mouth. "Oh, my lord. Someone poisoned it? Why would they do that?"

"Maybe because they believed it would be used on your patients?" Dolfe offered.

The vet's expression was tight with fear. "Of course. That makes more sense than someone knowing Alicia was going to use the ointment on herself." She shook her head, "Maybe they'll go away now for good."

"Who?" Brita asked.

"The *Medical Restitution League*." Amanda seemed surprised Brita would ask. "They're the obvious suspects if my clients were the target."

Brita didn't comment on that observation one way or the other.

"What about Ms. Prince's boyfriend?" Dolfe asked.

"I don't know much about him." Amanda shrugged.

"Did they seem to get along?"

"I have no idea. He's come by to pick her up several times but I've never met him. He waits in the car for her."

"Don't you find that strange," Brita asked.

"Not really. Alicia said he was shy." Amanda took a deep, shuddering breath, her eyes filling with tears again. She watched as her dead technician was zipped into a body bag and strapped onto the gurney. "I can't believe she's gone."

"We'll figure this out, Mandy," Brita told her, reaching out to squeeze the vet's arm. "In the meantime, you should probably close the clinic."

She looked alarmed. "For how long?"

"It will have to be closed at least long enough to test all of your medical supplies. You don't want to poison anyone else by mistake."

The young vet deflated right before Dolfe's eyes. "I didn't think of that." She fixed Brita with a teary gaze. "This is going to ruin me."

"No, it's not. You have lots of friends and we're all going to pitch in to help."

Amanda nodded, sniffling. But she didn't look convinced.

Brita glanced at Dolfe and he nodded, moving away as he dialed his cousin, Godric. The phone rang several times, and he finally left a message. "Hey cuz, I need your help with something. Call me back."

Dolfe disconnected and caught Blaise's eye. She'd been on the phone for most of the morning and looked decidedly frazzled. He gathered from the forced patience in her voice that Doctor Willis' patients weren't very happy about having their appointments canceled.

She rubbed her eyes, nodding. "Okay, Mrs. Taggert. We'll talk to you soon." Blaise listened for a beat, rolled her eyes and then held the phone away from her ear. A high-pitched voice filled the air, clearly angry. Blaise put the phone back to her ear just long enough to chirp happily into it. "Have a nice day." She disconnected and drooped to the desk, her forehead resting against a pile of patient folders. "Just shoot me now."

"I take it people aren't happy about being postponed?"

Blaise lifted her head, sighing. "I can't really blame them. First those jerks with the signs and now a murder. I'm afraid we're going to lose a lot of patients because of this."

Dolfe moved behind her chair and put his hands on her shoulders, kneading some of the tension from them. "If they leave, they leave. Nothing can be done about that. In the meantime, we have more serious problems."

She groaned softly as he eased the stiffness from her neck and shoulders. But his words brought her head back up. "What did you find out?"

"We think Alicia used an ointment that was laced with poison. Which means the clinic needs to shut down until everything is tested."

Blaise closed her eyes. "Oh my gosh. That's going to take forever and be really expensive."

Dolfe gave her shoulders a final squeeze. "I have some ideas on how to help with that. In the meantime, tell me about this morning."

"Not much to tell, really. I got here about seven thirty. Ivy and I came inside and went upstairs. I was supposed to meet with Mandy."

He nodded. "About the flu clinic."

"Yeah." Her eyes went wide. "I almost forgot! There was a car at the old groomer's building when I got here. I tried to talk to the driver, to find out what he was doing over there, but he laid rubber getting out of here."

Dolfe expelled air. "It's a good thing you didn't approach that car, Blaise. You could have been a victim too."

"You think Alicia's murderer was in the car? Why would he hang around?"

"You were here an hour before the clinic opens. He'd have thought he had time."

"Do we know TOD?"

Dolfe almost smiled. She'd been hanging around with him for too long. She threw out the lingo like a pro. "We won't have a definitive time of death until the ME gets her on the table, but from what we could see she was killed sometime last night, probably around midnight."

"Then it's unlikely the car had anything to do with it. I can't imagine a murderer hanging around for seven hours after killing someone."

"No. Unless he or she had other stuff to do before leaving." He arched a brow, letting her decipher his meaning.

He knew when she understood by the sudden widening of her eyes. "Oh no."

It would probably take some time to poison all of Amanda's medical supplies if that was the killer's goal.

Brita and Mandy came out just then, keeping them from discussing the ugly possibilities the young vet probably had yet to fully consider.

If Alicia Prince's death was the result of medical supply poisoning, there was a very good chance that her death wasn't the real goal of the killer.

And if that was the case, a whole bunch of beloved pets could be targets, and their unfortunate single murder could very rapidly become widespread euthanization of a lot of innocent pets.

3

"Where do we start?" Blaise asked Brita later, standing next to her rusted sedan in the clinic parking lot.

Brita arched a brow. "We?"

Blaise's temper spiked. "I've worked side by side with Alicia Prince for three months. I know you're going to use Dolfe for legwork. You might as well get used to the idea that he and I go together. We're a package deal."

"Like carrots and peas in a chicken pot pie," he said, nodding. "I'm thinking of renaming my company to include her." He lifted a hand, sliding it across the air, theatrically. "Brawn and Beauty Investigations."

"How about Beauty and the Beast?" Blaise offered helpfully.

He dropped an arm around her shoulders.

"Don't be so hard on yourself, honey. I wouldn't call you a beast exactly. Except maybe when you're hangry."

Blaise smacked him on the shoulder.

Shaking her head, Brita grabbed the handle of the car door. "I'll let you two battle that one out. Personally, I think Pot Pie Investigations works."

"We'll mind your Peas and Carrots?" Dolfe offered with a frown.

"Bring us your half-baked problems..." Blaise added with a frown. "Needs work."

"Start with her friends and family," Brita said, sliding into her car.

Dolfe frowned. "That would be a strange slogan for a PI business."

Brita gave him a look. "Alicia Prince. Try to focus, Honeybun."

"Oh. Right." He grinned.

"You'll check out the car I saw?" Blaise asked.

"It would help if you'd gotten a license plate number."

"There was a one, I think. And a G. Not necessarily in that order."

"So, a black or darkish car, two or four-door, old but maybe new with possibly a one and or a G in the license plate? Piece of cake."

Blaise grimaced. "I recognize that my observational skills might need a bit of work."

"Maybe just a titch." Brita grinned. "If you're

going to be the peas to Dolfe's carrot you might want to work on that."

Dolfe and Blaise snorted and Brita paled, realizing how her innocent reference had sounded. "Lord help me."

"I think we've got our slogan," Dolfe said.

Yetta Prince hunched on the edge of a blue leather couch, her narrow shoulders rounded forward and her face in her hands. She hadn't stopped crying since Dolfe and Blaise arrived.

Dolfe handed her a spotless white hankie. "We're so sorry for your loss."

Yetta took his hankie and loudly blew her nose, swiping it over the red and swollen area a few times before dropping her hands back to her lap.

"I just can't believe someone killed her. I mean... it's not like she had a dangerous job or something."

Blaise leaned forward, patting the older woman on a bony knee. "She loved her job. And I've never seen anybody who was a better vet tech than Alicia."

Yetta sniffed loudly, nodding. "She did love it."

"Mrs. Prince, can you think of anyone who might have wanted to hurt your daughter?"

"No. Everybody loved Alicia. She had tons of

friends. Just check her Facebook page. She was very popular."

"Was there anybody new in her life? Any new boyfriends or someone she mentioned as having behaved strangely?"

To her credit, despite clear emotional devastation, Yetta Prince gave his question careful thought before answering. "I can't think of anybody."

"Was she acting normally?"

Yetta frowned, staring at the wadded up hankie in her fist. Then she sighed. "She had been a little jumpy lately. I didn't think much about it. Alicia could be moody at times."

"Did she have a boyfriend?" Dolfe asked.

Mrs. Prince shoved a bright red strand of hair off her pale face. "She did. In fact, he was her first since the divorce."

Dolfe straightened slightly. "She was divorced?"

"Yes. A year ago." Yetta frowned. "It definitely wasn't amicable. They fought over the dog. He was really angry that Alicia ended up with him. I guess you could take a look at Roger for the mur..." Yetta swallowed hard, shaking her head.

They all looked at the big Great Dane splayed over the charcoal gray carpeting. He was a beauty, but the white hairs around his muzzle and his laziness told Blaise he was a mature dog.

"I'll want you to write the ex-husband's name,

address and phone number down for us," Dolfe said gently.

"Of course."

"Tell us about Alicia's new boyfriend."

Yetta gave a little frown before she forced a smile. "He seems nice."

"What's his name?" Blaise asked, returning the smile.

"Peter Fawcett. He's a lawyer. I think she told me he works downtown, somewhere around Monument Circle."

"How did he treat your daughter, Mrs. Prince?" Dolfe asked.

Yetta frowned. "Okay, I guess. I've only met him a couple of times. They came to Sunday dinner." Her grin widened. "He loved my roast. He told me his mom used to make it just like I do, with the baby carrots and new potatoes." Yetta brushed a hand over the couch, skimming some dog hairs off the glossy surface. "He lost his parents a few years back, I guess. I think he has a brother."

"Did Alicia seem happy? Were they getting along, okay?"

Mrs. Prince flinched slightly. "You don't think Peter...?"

"It's all part of the investigative process," Dolfe interrupted gently. "We're just gathering information right now."

The older woman nodded. "Alicia was very

happy. They spent every free minute together, and he even took her shopping a few times." She gave them a sad smile. "Not too many men will go shopping with their gals. I took that to mean he was smitten." She shook her head, sniffing loudly. "They seemed like a perfect match."

"Mrs. Prince, could you give us Roger's information now? Then we'll get out of your hair."

The older woman stood up and headed into the kitchen. Bart the Dane leaped to his feet with an agility belying his age and size and plodded after her.

Blaise hoped the big dog would be company for the woman, maybe ease the pain of her daughter's loss.

A moment later Mrs. Prince returned, handing Dolfe a small sheet of paper with a name and address scribbled across the surface. "I'm afraid I don't have his cell phone number. He got rid of his landline a few months ago."

"This is very helpful." Dolfe touched Blaise's arm and she rose when he did. On an impulse, she reached out and gave the woman a quick hug. "Your daughter was a good woman, Yetta. She was so gentle to the animals at the clinic and so kind to the owners. She'll be deeply missed."

Yetta Prince nodded, fresh tears filling her light blue eyes. "Thank you for saying that, dear. It means a lot."

They said their goodbyes and headed for Dolfe's truck. Blaise looped her arm through his and laid her head on his shoulder. "It must be so sad to lose your child."

He kissed her forehead. "I can't even imagine." Dolfe opened the door of his truck and gave her a hand up, closing the door behind her and hurrying around.

They drove in silence for a few minutes, both touched by Yetta Prince's pain. Then Dolfe turned to her, grinning. "We should have gotten a picture of that Dane sleeping. Clovis would be relieved to see they actually do snooze occasionally."

Blaise giggled. Dolfe's cousin Clovis Honeybun had a four-month-old Great Dane puppy named Darth Dane. The puppy was the cutest thing Blaise had ever seen, aside from her own two fur babies, and he was just about as sweet as he could be. But the enormous baby never stopped moving. And he gave her own puppy Badly a run for his money in the family contest for naughtiest dog.

"Do you want to eat some lunch before we go talk to the ex?"

She widened her eyes. "You have to ask?"

Dolfe shook his head. "You pick."

"Something fast. How about that new stuffed potato place?"

"Sold."

On the way to the restaurant, they drove past a

small brick building with a large white sign proclaiming it an emergency animal clinic. There was a crowd outside, and many of the people milling around held familiar signs.

"Those jerks sure do get around," Blaise said frowning. The *Medical Restitution League* was apparently focusing on another unsuspecting veterinarian business for the moment.

Dolfe slowed the truck, frowning. "I wish your friend Mandy had security cameras. I'd be willing to bet those people had something to do with Alicia Prince's death."

"If they did, we'll figure it out."

He turned to her and gave her a smile. "You have a lot of faith in our abilities."

"Of course. Am I not the peas to your carrot?"

He snorted out a laugh. "She's never going to live that one down."

"No, she's not," Blaise told him with a laugh. "I'll make sure of it."

Dolfe's cell rang. He glanced at it before answering. "It's Brita." Dolfe punched the *Answer* button and hit speaker. "Hey, Brit. You have both of us."

"All the vegetables," Blaise said.

There was a beat of silence, then an unmistakable sigh. "I suppose it's too much to ask that you don't tell your cousins about that?"

Their response was to laugh.

"That's what I thought. Well first, I hate you so much. And second, I have cause of death."

"And?"

"It was poison as we suspected. But that doesn't point to Alicia Prince being the intended target."

"You think the radicals poisoned the ointment to hurt some of Dr. Mandy's patients?"

"That's where I'm leaning. It's just too much of a coincidence that they were stalking the place and this happened. Plus, we dug up another case in Minnesota. A large animal hospital where a tube of Phenylbutazone was spiked and ended up killing an elderly horse with laminitis."

"Lami-whatis?" Blaise asked.

"Pain in the hooves," Dolfe explained, frowning. "I've used it on Noire a few times."

Dolfe had a beautiful Friesian horse which he kept south of Indianapolis at his cousin Peyton's dude ranch.

"I'm guessing the radicals were present at the Minnesota vet?"

"Yes."

"When did this happen?"

"About two months ago. No arrests have been made yet, but it's just too much of a coincidence." There was a beat of silence and then Brita went on. "My sergeant's pressuring me to focus only on the MRL for this. Unfortunately, if we can pin it on them they'll probably be able to plead down to manslaughter."

"That's terrible!" Blaise exclaimed. "Alicia Prince is dead. Whoever's responsible for this should be thrown in prison for life."

"I don't disagree, Blaise. But we need to work within the system."

Blaise shook her head, so angry she could spit nails.

Dolfe reached over and squeezed her hand. "I've got a few names I'm going to follow up on."

"Do that. Sarge hasn't told me to stop investigating all leads. He just made it clear we were going after the *League*. He's going to make a statement to the press later today."

"That actually might help us," Dolfe said. "If the radicals start feeling some heat they might back down. And nobody will expect us to be looking at other possibilities. Maybe we can slide in under the radar."

"Maybe. I'll give you shade as long as I can."

"Thanks, Brit. We'll touch base later and let you know what we find out."

4

*R*oger Jacks was riding a lawnmower over his massive lawn when they pulled into his drive. He was wearing sound-deadening head-phones and was pointed away from the driveway so he didn't know Dolfe and Blaise were there for a couple of minutes. When he saw them, his head came up and he frowned, slicing a finger across his throat and pointing toward this mailbox, where a big "No Trespassing" sign warned visitors he wasn't interested.

Dolfe leaned back against his truck and crossed his arms over his chest.

Jacks headed toward him at full speed, a glower painting his ruddy face. He stopped a mere three feet away from Dolfe's boots, yanking off the head-phones. "Can't you people read?"

Dolfe waited a beat, looking down his long,

straight nose at the angry homeowner, and then eased his PI license from his shirt pocket. "Dolfe Honeybun, Private Investigator. This is Blaise Runa, my associate."

Blaise lifted her hand and wiggled her fingers. "Hey. Nice lawn."

The man stared at her as if he wasn't sure whether she was a weed or a flower and then shook his head. "Thanks. But you still need to leave."

"I'm working with the *Indianapolis Metropolitan Police Department* as a consultant."

"What exactly do you consult about?"

"A little bit of this. A little bit of that."

The two men locked eyes and commenced a battle of irritated gazes. Blaise checked the polish on her nails. It was looking a little worn. She'd have to give herself a manicure later. Finally, when she figured they'd had plenty of time to compare inches and thump their chests, Blaise decided it was time for a woman's touch.

"Mr. Jacks, are you aware of what happened to Alicia?"

The man flinched as if struck. "I am."

"Well, we're here to try to find her killer. I assume you'd like to help with that."

Alicia Prince's ex pursed his lips, drawing Blaise's attention to what was probably his best feature. He was a good-looking man. Probably in his mid-thirties and, though a bit rounder in the middle than he should be, still in pretty good shape.

He looked like he could make Dolfe break a sweat. Though her honey would easily take him.

"I thought it was an accident."

Dolfe shrugged, offering the man his tried and true response for shutting down inappropriate questions. "We're still in the fact-gathering stage. Nothing's been determined for sure."

Jacks looked at Blaise. "But you said..."

Blaise shrugged, giving him an innocent smile.

Jacks shook his dark head and climbed off the mower. When he straightened to his full height, Blaise could see he was taller than she'd thought. He was probably close to six feet three inches. Big enough to cause somebody some trouble if he wanted to. "Alicia didn't take drugs," he told them gruffly.

"Not even the prescription kind?" Dolfe asked.

Jacks shrugged. "I wouldn't know about that. She didn't have any health issues when I knew her. Except for occasional lower back pain."

"Did she use anything for that?" Blaise asked, thinking of the ointment in the tech's hand.

"Aspirin sometimes. Occasionally she'd put that foul-smelling stuff on her back. I hated the smell of that stuff." He shuddered.

"Do you know if she ever used meds from the clinic?" Dolfe asked.

"Animal medicine?" He frowned. "Is that what killed her? I'd think she was smart enough not to use stuff made for dogs and cats."

"My understanding is that some of the meds are interchangeable," Dolfe said. "Like Phenylbutazone, for example. It used to be approved for human use. But now we mostly just use it for horses."

"Phenyl what?" Jacks leaned against his mower. "I have no idea what you're talking about."

Blaise believed him. He looked angry but not guilty. "Mr. Jacks, were you aware of anybody who might want to hurt your ex-wife?"

"I have no idea. I rarely speak..." He cleared his throat. "--spoke to her anymore."

"Because you were too angry?" Dolfe asked softly.

Jacks glowered at him. "Are you trying to insinuate that I killed Alicia?"

"You fought with her over the dog. You're clearly still mad about it."

"The custody battle was almost a year ago. I'm angry because..." He hesitated, his brows lowering as if he couldn't remember why he was mad. "To tell you the truth, being mad at Alicia has become something of a habit. She really wasn't a bad person."

"But you wanted your dog," Blaise offered gently.

Jacks sniffed, one hand finding his hip. "If that's all, I'm kind of busy."

"You never answered my question, Mr. Jacks," Dolfe prodded.

"Did I kill her? No, Mr. Honeybun. I didn't kill my ex-wife. Believe it or not, I loved Alicia. Not romantically. Not anymore. But we were friends long before we became lovers and I'd like to think we still were. I believe she feels...felt...the same way."

"Have you met her new boyfriend?" Dolfe asked.

Blaise expected Jacks to react to the painful question, but he didn't show any emotion. "No. I knew she was dating someone, but I had no desire to meet him. I'm sure I'd hate him if I did."

At least the man was honest.

Dolfe handed him a card. "If you hear anything that might help us..."

Jacks took the card, staring down at it for a long moment. Finally, he looked up. "Do you think I could get Bart back now." He glanced guiltily away when Dolfe fixed him with a speculative look. "I would never kill Alicia for the dog. But if she's gone...he might need me."

"We saw your dog," Blaise told him. "He seems comfortable and happy. And I think Mrs. Prince needs him now. I'd give her some time. Maybe when she's feeling stronger..."

He nodded. "Thanks. You're right. I'm being selfish. I should probably go see Yetta, tell her I'm here if she needs to talk."

"That would be good," Blaise agreed.

Peter Fawcett lived like a lawyer. He resided in an upper-middle-class neighborhood in Carmel, one of the most prestigious suburbs of Indianapolis. The man's house was a brick Colonial style with white pillars and a porch that ran the length of the front of the house.

The shutters on the home were black, and the railing along the porch was black wrought Iron.

It was a pretty home, surrounded by tidy flower beds that looked like they were professionally managed.

The driveway leading to the house was fairly long, curving gently toward a four-car garage that was attached to the home.

"Nice," Blaise breathed as they drove up and parked in front of the big garage.

Dolfe scanned a gaze over the house. It didn't seem like a killer's home.

Not that rich men had never been known to murder their lovers. But the way Alicia Prince had been killed didn't feel like a rich man's crime.

Of course, a *smart* rich man would look for exactly that perception when committing the crime of murder.

"Apparently Mr. Fawcett is doing well for himself." Blaise murmured.

Brita had looked into the man and learned that

he was a patent lawyer and came from a wealthy family of lawyers and doctors. A background that could certainly offer him the necessary resources to create the perfect crime.

Dolfe opened Blaise's door and gave her a handout.

"Thanks, future husband."

"You're welcome, honey."

He took her hand as they started along the softly curving sidewalk. The walkway was concrete bordered in brick that matched the house, and climbed a rounded set of front steps to the porch. Dolfe used the door knocker on the painted black wood door. Shrill barking commenced in response.

Dolfe heard the pitter pat of multiple paws coming from the other side of the door. "Sounds like Ivy and Badly," he remarked.

Blaise grinned.

A man's voice appeared amidst the yapping. "Back, ladies," the voice said. The door opened, showing them a decent looking guy around six feet tall, with red-rimmed light brown eyes and disheveled dark blond hair. He wore baggy sweats with food stains on the front, and his feet were bare on the slate tile floor.

Two fat little Corgis danced impatiently at his feet, their eyes bright with happy welcome.

"Can I help you?"

"Mr. Fawcett?" Dolfe extended his hand. "I'm

Dolfe Honeybun and this is my associate, Blaise. I'm a consultant with the police."

He frowned. "The police? What do they want with me?"

"We'd just like to ask you a few questions about Alicia," Blaise offered with a disarming smile. "I actually worked with her at *Precious Pets*."

Fawcett took a closer look at her. "Blaise. Yes, I think Alicia mentioned you." He shook his head, his lips quivering as his haunted gaze turned glossy with unshed tears. "Come in, please. You don't mind dogs, do you? These two are harmless, but they think everyone deserves their love and attention."

Blaise looked down at the two cuties, grinning as they licked her ankles below her jeans and above her flats. "We have two of our own. They pretty much have the same attitude."

"Small dogs?" Fawcett asked.

"Yes."

He nodded, closing the door behind them. "Little dogs have attitudes that are bigger than they are. It's one of the things I like about them."

Dolfe let that sink in. He'd been struggling with misgivings about being a red-blooded male with two tiny dogs...not wanting to be confused with a metrosexual type guy...but Fawcett's observation was interesting. He did like Ivy and Badly's "take no prisoners" attitude.

Fawcett pointed toward a door at the side of the

wide entryway. "Let's talk in my office. It's more comfortable."

The home was just as elegant on the inside as it was on the exterior. The dark slate floors of the entry were dissected in the center by a curving staircase with a floating banister, leading to an opulent second floor, with golden sconces on the walls and thick, creamy carpeting on the floors.

The wide entranceway on the left lead to an enormous living area with light wood floors and thick oriental carpets.

It definitely didn't have a lived-in look. Dolfe would be afraid to touch anything in the home.

But he felt right at home in Peter Fawcett's study, which was comfortably cluttered and filled with books of all sizes and genres, including hardbacks with gilded lettering as well as well-used paperbacks.

Fawcett sat down on a long couch in front of a gas fireplace that wasn't lit. He indicated the matching armchairs across from him, gathering up a newspaper and folding it before setting it on the marble-topped coffee table between them. "I'm sorry for the mess. I haven't been myself since I heard."

"It's been a real shock," Blaise told him. "I still can't believe she's gone."

He frowned, sitting back and staring at the table with unseeing eyes.

"Mr. Fawcett, do you know of any reason Alicia might have been killed?"

The man blinked rapidly. He shuffled his feet and glanced away, seemingly unwilling to meet Dolfe's gaze. Probably because of the tears sparkling in his eyes. "I couldn't possibly imagine. The only thing I can think is that it was some kind of accident." His gaze jerked to Blaise. "Do the police have a cause of death yet?"

"I don't think so, no. But she was holding a tube of ointment in one hand. Antibiotic cream."

Fawcett nodded. "She liked that stuff. I'm afraid Alicia cut her arm the other day doing yard work. The ointment took the pain out very quickly and was speeding the healing. It's actually great stuff. I've been trying to figure out how to get some for myself." He looked down at the two corgis, who were playing well-mannered bitey face at his feet.

Fawcett was quiet for a beat and then looked up. "Dr. Willis isn't mad about her using it is she?"

"Not at all," Blaise assured him with a smile. "I guess it was pretty common practice at the clinic."

"Wait, are you telling me the police think she was poisoned with that stuff? How is that possible? Alicia would have known if it was toxic to humans. She went to vet school. The only reason she didn't finish was because she ran out of money for school." Fawcett reached up and scratched his jaw, looking genuinely perplexed.

Blaise cocked her head. "I didn't know that. Alicia never told me."

"She wouldn't. She was ashamed about not finishing. I told her that was ridiculous but..." He shrugged. "Our emotions and feelings aren't always rational, are they?"

"Almost never," Blaise agreed with a smile. "She was very good with the animals. Dr. Willis relied on her for a lot."

"Yes. She would have made an excellent veterinarian."

"Do you have any idea why Alicia was at the clinic after everyone else left?" Dolfe asked him.

Fawcett shifted his feet away from the playing dogs and tugged on his ear. "She'd called me and said she wasn't quite ready to come home and that she'd phone back when she was. I think it was around six o'clock. But then she heard a noise and was going to check on it."

"What did she hear?" Dolfe asked, sitting forward.

"She thought one of the dogs in recovery was banging on its kennel. Nothing too alarming."

Dolfe and Blaise shared a look. "Do you know which dog?" Blaise asked.

"It was a wolfhound. Agnes was her name. Alicia loved that dog. She loved the bigger dogs."

Dolfe nodded. "We met her dog, Bart when we spoke to her mom."

"Bart's great," Fawcett agreed with a sad smile.

Dolfe suddenly realized Blaise had gone quiet and he turned to her. Her expression was filled with alarm. "What's wrong, honey?"

Blaise lifted a finger and grabbed her cell phone. She dialed quickly and, a beat later, spoke into the phone. "Hey, Jenny. Can you tell me the current status of Agnes? Yeah, the wolfhound." Blaise listened for a moment and then turned to Dolfe. Her gaze was filled with alarm. "Are you sure?"

"You need to check on her. We need verification. Yes! Please, it's important. Thanks." Waiting for the person on the other end to return, Blaise skimmed Dolfe a glance. "I thought Agnes went home. We all did."

He realized immediately what she was telling him. The kennel where Alicia had been left was empty except for Alicia's body. If the dog had been in that kennel before the murder, where had she gone?

"Yes, I'm still here. Okay." Blaise scrubbed a hand over her face. "Oh no. This is bad. Well, then she's missing, and we need to find her."

5

"Why didn't they know the dog was missing?" Dolfe asked Blaise the next morning at breakfast.

"Her owners had planned to pick her up the day before yesterday but got waylaid out of town and called to ask the clinic to keep her another night."

"So, again, why didn't they know..."

"Because the owners spoke to Alicia," Blaise interrupted with a frown. "She did note it in the dog's chart, but nobody had a reason to look for it. When we saw that Alicia had been stuffed into the kennel, we didn't even think about the dog that was supposed to be inside of it. We all thought Agnes had gone home the night before."

"Any ideas where she is?" Brita asked.

"Not yet. We've got people putting flyers out and the local news has shown pictures of her several times. The owners are offering a pretty sizeable award."

Brita shoved her plate away, wiping her lips as she swallowed her last bite of toast. The local diner-type restaurant where they were having breakfast was starting to thin out. When they'd arrived an hour earlier it had been filled to the brim and so noisy they could barely carry on a conversation.

Blaise pushed her eggs around, too anxious to eat. "The missing dog changes things. Maybe she was stolen for some reason and Alicia just got caught in the crossfire."

Brita shook her head. "I wish it did. The media is claiming the *Medical Restitution League* took the dog to make a point. I got the word last night. I'm still supposed to keep focusing on the radicals."

"Is there anything in MRL's past activities that would suggest the missing dog might be their doing?" Dolfe asked.

"Not a whisper." Brita stared at her coffee cup, looking as unhappy as Blaise felt.

"You don't believe the radicals killed Alicia, do you?" Blaise asked her friend.

Brita shrugged. "I'm withholding judgment."

"Stop being a cop for two seconds, Brit," Blaise snapped. "Tell me what your gut is saying."

Brita sighed. "I'm not convinced they're behind it, no. But you have to admit the evidence all seems to point to them."

Blaise shook her head. "Alicia's mom said she'd been nervous lately, jumpy. What if someone was threatening her?"

"But who?" Brita asked. "And why?"

Blaise frowned.

"Find some evidence I can work with, girlfriend. Then I'll help you follow it up. Even if it doesn't make the higher-ups happy."

Blaise nodded. "That's fair."

Brita looked at Dolfe. "What did you think about the victim's ex and boyfriend?"

"I think her ex is more pragmatic than devastated. And I think her boyfriend is hiding something."

Blaise blinked in surprise. "You do?"

"He gave me several guilt markers when I asked him about potential suspects. I think he suspects someone he and or Alicia knew killed her."

"If that's true, he must have a good reason to protect that person."

"Maybe he's been threatened too," Blaise offered.

"Or he cares about the killer."

Brita settled her mug onto the table. "His brother?"

"It's worth looking into. What do you know about him?"

"Honestly? I haven't had time to do background on him. The little bit of information I have would seem to refute the idea he's involved. I think the poor man's dying of cancer."

"Oh," Blaise frowned. "That's horrible. No wonder Peter Fawcett's upset. He's already lost his girlfriend and is in danger of losing his brother."

Dolfe sat quietly, his big hands wrapped around his own mug. When he didn't respond, Brita tapped the table with a fingernail. "Honeybun? What are you thinking?"

He flashed her a quick look. "You won't like it. Even *I* don't like it."

"I don't like anything about any of this."

"What do you know about Fawcett's insurance situation?"

She stared at him for a long moment, then understanding lit her gaze. "Ah. You're thinking the dying brother might be involved in MRL?"

Shrugging, Dolfe pulled out his wallet, extracting a credit card. "We need to look at it. Cancer drugs can be really expensive. If his insurance is limiting or excluding the necessary drugs..."

Brita nodded. "I get the gist of what you're thinking. That's prime ground for the radicals to plow." She frowned. "There's something else you should know. I was curious as to why the higher-ups were being so political about this case. It turns out Kelly Carter is trying to get a bill passed that would circumvent some of the FDA's control over human drugs."

"That's our new US Representative right?" Blaise asked. "I'm surprised he's rocking the boat already."

"It was one of his campaign promises," Brita said.

"That's huge," Dolfe said. "If people could make the decision to try experimental therapies themselves, lots of people could be saved."

"Or lots could die." Brita shrugged. "Don't get me wrong. I think it's only right that people should be able to decide for themselves whether they want to take the risk or not. It's just that there will be an uproar the first time someone dies."

"I'm guessing cost wouldn't be an issue with an experimental drug," Blaise offered. "A lot of them are still in the testing phase. Dini and I were talking about it the other day. She's been struggling to walk the fine line with her homemade remedies. She knows all about the FDA."

Nodding, Brita threw a twenty down on the table, near the check. "I'm buying."

Shoving her money back at her, Dolfe gathered up the bill and stood. "Keep your money. I got this."

"You always buy," Brita argued.

He shrugged. "So? I like to buy my two favorite ladies breakfast. Sue me." He walked away before Brita could argue any more.

She and Blaise shared a look. "He's very stubborn."

"He is," Blaise agreed. "But it looks good on him."

Brita's lips twitched on a grin. "Yeah, only a Honeybun could make such an ugly trait look good."

~

The clinic was still closed when they arrived. Dolfe spotted a mud-covered Range Rover in the parking lot. "Godric and Dini are here."

Blaise smiled. "Good. Mandy's gonna be so pumped. She's been wanting to open a holistic practice on the side."

There was no one in the lobby when they came inside the building. Midnight Joe was perched on Blaise's desk, bathing his big paws. He looked up and squinted his pretty green eyes at them, meowing softly.

Blaise scratched his head. "Mornin' Joe."

Dolfe and Blaise followed the sound of voices in the back room, finding the two vet techs, Adam and Jenny, along with Mandy Willis standing with two visitors around a stainless-steel exam table.

The man was over six feet tall and had gray eyes, longish dark red hair and a sexy stubble on his square chin. The woman was stunning, her creamy brown skin showing her mixed African and Native American heritage, and her waist-length black hair smoothed back into a low ponytail that showed off her high cheekbones and dark, nearly black eyes.

The surface of the table was filled with an assortment of jars and bottles with labels designed in earthy colors featuring Dini's dream catcher logo.

Everyone turned as they came into the room. Godric offered Dolfe his hand, and Dini gave Blaise a quick hug. "I'm so sorry for your loss," she told Blaise gently.

"Thank you," Blaise responded, hugging her back. "And thanks for coming to help."

Godric grinned. "Are you kidding me, she's so excited to share her new line."

"I am!" Dini exclaimed without embarrassment. "I've been testing it out on everybody and their pets." She laughed good-naturedly. "Now I have a whole new batch of test subjects."

Mandy frowned and Blaise hurried to reassure her. "Don't worry, Dini's a perfectionist. She says *test* but she really means improve on near perfection. I've tried her ointments. They're amazing."

Dolfe raised his hand. "Me too. The willow bark ointment took my shoulder pain away almost immediately. The stuff's magic."

Mandy grinned. "I can't wait to try it. I have a few older dogs with debilitating arthritis that could really use something like that."

"No side-effects?" Jenny asked, frowning.

Blaise knew that Jenny didn't trust holistic medicine. Apparently, her mother had been cheated by a fake chiropractor once, and it had done severe damage to the woman's health. Since then, Jenny had ruthlessly applied her dislike for non-traditional medical care to all forms. Including the Eastern and Native American kind, which, as Blaise understood it, had been proven to be very effective.

Dini shook her head. "Nothing so far. But that's one of the reasons I want to keep testing. If there's a weakness somewhere, I want to know so I can address it."

Jenny didn't respond. Her frown stayed in place and she had her arms crossed over her flat chest in a classic closed posture.

Blaise wasn't worried. She had confidence Dini would win the woman over. Or rather, her holistic medicines would do it. They were just that good.

Godric led Dolfe away from the group. A moment later, Blaise heard him ask about the tainted medicines. Dolfe had asked him to come and test all of Mandy's existing supply to make sure they weren't poisoned. It was a huge favor and Mandy was really grateful. If she'd had to replace all the meds or get them tested at a lab, it would have set her back much more than she could easily recoup.

Blaise joined the two men. "I'll get you set up with all the equipment you need. The lab's right through here."

The morning sped by and, before Blaise knew it, Adam was asking for her lunch order. She looked up from the chart she was updating for Jenny and smiled. "I didn't realize it was getting that late."

He sighed. "It's been a crazy morning. Things just don't run quite as well without Alicia."

"No. She was a great office manager. Do you think Mandy will slide one of you into the job?" She suspected the answer was no. Jenny and Adam were great vet techs, but they couldn't manage the day-to-day aspects of running an efficient practice.

Blaise wanted to get his perspective on things moving forward.

"Not a chance," Adam said without equivocation. "I don't have the skill to run an office, and Jenny doesn't have the...imagination."

Blaise knew what he meant. Jenny was a little set in her ways. She had trouble stepping out of her comfort zone or thinking creatively to solve problems. Both things Alicia had been especially good at doing. "Any idea who Mandy might hire for the position?"

Adam leaned close, lowering his voice. "There's a woman at Badgersville. She'd be perfect, and she hates her boss. I think her name's Billy. She's the one I expect to take the job."

Blaise nodded, hesitating a beat before jumping into the subject she really wanted to broach.

Adam waved his lunch list. "Lunch?"

"Oh, a cobb salad, please." She closed the patient

file she'd been working on. "I just can't believe someone might have killed Alicia."

Adam hesitated just long enough to make Blaise think he might have information he hadn't shared. "What is it? Do you know something?"

He glanced quickly around. "Just that I saw her fighting with some guy in the parking lot the other day. It looked pretty serious."

"Did you hear what they were fighting about?"

Adam shrugged. "Not really. Just a word here or there. But the guy seemed really aggressive with Alicia. He kept stepping closer, poking his finger at her."

Blaise let her eyebrows lift. "What did she do?"

"She finally slapped at his hand and walked away. He started to go after her but I stepped out from between a couple of cars and, when he saw me, he stopped. He jumped in his car and left, squealing out of the parking lot."

"That's terrifying. I wonder if he's the guy who...you know."

"Could be, I guess. But probably not. I think they were just having a regular fight about something stupid." He laughed. "Like leaving the lid off the toothpaste or something."

"Oh," Blaise blinked. "You think they were lovers?"

"Lovers? That's probably too pretty a word for what I saw but, yeah, maybe."

"So, it was Alicia's boyfriend, Peter?"

"Not Peter, no. Some other guy."

"You're sure?"

"Positive. Have you met Peter?"

Blaise nodded.

"Then you'll understand. Think polar opposite. This guy was the lumberjack to Peter's metrosexual."

"Can you describe him?"

"Big guy, probably around six feet and kind of burly. He had big forearms, like Popeye." Adam laughed. "All he needed was an anchor tattoo." Shaking his head, he lifted a hand. "I'd better get this ordered. Mandy's got a surgery in an hour."

"Yeah thanks, Adam." Blaise watched him walk away from the desk and remembered something else she needed to ask. "Hey, Adam?"

He turned, irritation briefly coloring his expression. "Yeah?"

"What kind of car was the guy driving?"

His face cleared and he grinned. "Every man's dream car. It was a black 2001 BMW M5. The coolest car ever made."

6

*B*laise squinted at the image of the car on the screen. "I guess the BMW Adam mentioned could have been the car I saw."

Dolfe eyed her, concerned she wasn't more sure. "How well did you see the car?"

"You mean my stellar description wasn't enough of a clue?"

"I guess it should have been."

She shoved back from the computer, rubbing a hand wearily over her eyes. "We're just spinning our wheels here."

He grabbed her hand, kissing the palm. "We're moving through the steps of the investigation. There's no giant arrow that pops up, pointing to the killer. Unfortunately."

"But I might have actually *seen* the killer's car. We

could find him right now if I'd noticed more. A license plate or...something."

"You got more than most other people would have, honey. Don't be so hard on yourself."

Blaise frowned, looking down at the keyboard. The tiny bundle in her lap stirred, stretching his stubby legs and yawning widely.

Blaise's eyes popped wide. "Oh, oh. It's waking up."

Dolfe chuckled. "Let me take him. You go, have a long, hot bath. It'll make you feel better."

Blaise lifted Badly and kissed the top of his soft head. "You be a good boy for daddy."

The puppy licked the end of her nose and then bit it.

Blaise yelped in surprise. "You little..."

Badly wriggled happily as Dolfe grabbed him away from her. "Are you okay?"

"Of course. He doesn't bite hard. He's just a little rascal." She grinned as she watched the two of them heading for the door. The puppy's tail snapped the air behind Dolfe's elbow and his gaze lifted adoringly as Dolfe scolded him in a soft tone that wouldn't scare or do anything at all to train the naughty puppy.

The two boys were bonding nicely.

She stood up. "Come on, Miss Ivy." The little dog jumped up from her throne-shaped bed, immediately interested in their next adventure. "Let's go have some girl time."

Blaise ran the water as hot as she could stand it and poured sweet smelling bubbles into it. Miss Ivy circled three times and then curled up on Blaise's towel on the floor, sighing contentedly.

Blaise lay back in the soapy heat and sighed with her own contentment. Dolfe was right, as usual. A bath was just what she needed. She did her best thinking in the tub.

Letting her thoughts sort themselves out, Blaise ran a mental list of everything they knew. It wasn't much, and the pieces didn't appear to fit together at all, but somehow they would. She just needed to figure out how.

Alicia had been acting strangely lately.

She had a new boyfriend, but not brand new. So, he probably wasn't the direct cause of her strange behavior.

Peter Fawcett seemed genuinely upset about her death. But not upset enough to tell them what he was hiding. He probably wouldn't be protecting Alicia since she was beyond caring. Which meant he was protecting someone else. But who?

His brother? They needed to check him out. If for no other reason than just to tick him off the list. If he truly was sick without the means to pay for meds, that would be a powerful motivation for murder.

Brita's bombshell of that morning still bothered Blaise. If there's a member of Congress who's trying to get a bill passed to allow human pharmaceuticals to be used on a trial basis without first getting FDA approval, that would be huge. And the *Medical Restitution League* might double down on its efforts to make sure that law got passed. The question was, would those efforts include murder?

Blaise sure would like to talk to Representative Carter. She'd like to know if he's being influenced by MRL. Then she realized she could easily do that. Dolfe's dad was a US Senator. If Brick Honeybun couldn't get them an appointment with Carter, nobody could.

Blaise felt better after that.

Until she remembered sweet, giant Agnes. She really hoped the beautiful dog hadn't become a victim in MRL's battle for medical restitution.

Her gaze fell on Ivy and her stomach tightened with fear. If the group was willing to harm a dog as sweet and daunting as the big wolfhound, what would they do to a tiny mutt with big ears and way too much 'tude?

The thought took the fun right out of her bath. And made her want to grab up both her pets and never let them out of her sight.

J enny and Adam were looking kind of dour when Blaise came in the next morning with Ivy in tow. The two techs looked up and their eyes went wide in a silent message. She could hear Mandy's voice coming from the office and it sounded strained.

"What's going on?" Blaise asked quietly. She set the box of donuts she'd brought on top of the desk but, to her vast surprise, neither of the usually ravenous techs reached for one.

"Ralph Bickers is here," Jenny said with a roll of her brown eyes. "He's trying to scare Mandy into selling to him."

"But that's crazy. Why would she do that?"

Adam shrugged. "Everybody's pretty squigged out about Alicia getting murdered in the back room."

"Well yeah, of course. But nobody's going to hold that against Mandy, right?"

Both techs were silent. Jenny chewed her bottom lip, her gaze worried.

"What?" Blaise asked. Ivy snuffled around the desk and tugged on the leash until Blaise let go. There were no other dogs in the waiting room so Ivy was free to wander around.

Midnight Joe was perched on top of the water cooler in the corner, peering smugly down at Ivy as she wandered over and yipped at him.

"All our morning appointments have canceled," Adam told her. "One lady said she just couldn't imagine coming in here now, knowing it was the scene of a murder."

Blaise felt her stomach twist with dread. Could Alicia's murder be the ruin of Mandy's practice?

"Stupid media," she finally murmured. The local news had been wall-to-wall coverage of the murder because everyone was trying to tie it to Representative Carter's new bill.

I've told you a hundred times, Ralph, I'm not interested!

The shrill tone of Mandy's usually chipper voice told Blaise it was time to intervene. She looked at the two techs. "Get on the phone and call everyone who canceled, tell them their office visit today is free if they show up."

"But..." Jenny started to argue.

"Just do it!" Blaise gave them a smile of apology. "We need to be proactive right now."

Adam nodded, a small smile playing over his lips. "It's genius."

Blaise headed toward Mandy's office. She called for Ivy as she headed down the short hall leading toward the back of the building, where Mandy kept an excruciatingly tidy office. She knocked quickly and opened the door before Mandy responded. Sticking her head inside the office, she gave her favorite vet a bright smile. "Good Morning. I was wondering if you'd like a donut." Blaise turned toward the short, widely made man standing on the other side of Mandy's desk and blinked, feigning surprise. "Doctor Bickers, I'm sorry. I didn't know you were here." Blaise moved into the office, closing the door behind Ivy as the little dog bounced inside and jumped up on Mandy's lap.

"Was Mandy telling you about her incredible idea?" Blaise looked from the frowning Bickers to her boss and nearly smiled at the confusion on Mandy's pretty face. But Mandy quickly hid her face in Ivy's fur.

Blaise cocked her head. "She didn't, did she? Girl, you're just too humble for your own good."

"What are you talking about?" Bickers grumbled.

"The clinic annex for canine flu patients. Mandy thought it would be a good idea to use the groomery as a temporary clinic to help infected dogs. We've just started discussing the details, but we were thinking that, for a fee, we could support the other vets in the area who've been turning away clients for fear of spreading the infection to the wider client population."

Despite himself, Bickers looked interested. "I wouldn't want my clients to come to you," he told Mandy in an accusatory tone.

"Of course not," she responded. "You'd have your own staff at the clinic. You'd bill your own patients and you'd keep all their records in your own office.

I'd just provide a safe space to treat the animals and charge a fee for use of the space. Though it might make sense to share personnel through all the participating vets so we don't have to bring those personnel back into our clinics. That would greatly reduce the chances of transmission for everybody."

Bickers frowned, but Blaise could see his mind spinning over the possibilities. Finally, he looked up at Mandy. "That might just work. It's been hard turning so many patients away, lately. But I couldn't risk infecting my entire client base."

"Yeah," Blaise agreed unhappily. "Those poor dogs have no place to go."

Bickers gave a short bark of a laugh. "Who cares about the stupid dogs. I've been losing revenue." He eyed Mandy, seemingly oblivious to the disgust in her expression. "I can't even imagine how this is affecting your business, what with a murder in the building and all. You might want to give serious consideration to selling out. You can pick up somewhere else and start over."

"Why would I do that?" Mandy asked him angrily.

"Where are your customers, this morning? Everyone's canceling on you, aren't they? People aren't going to want to come around now that you've had a murder in the building. They don't know if the killer is working here." He stared at Blaise until she bristled.

"Are you accusing me of murder?" she asked softly.

He shrugged. "It could have been any of you, couldn't it?"

Blaise opened her mouth to lay him out, but Mandy stood up, clutching Ivy against her chest like a binkie. Although Blaise recognized the signs of fear and worry in her friend's eyes, she took note of how the young vet straightened her shoulders and stiffened her spine against the older vet's attacks. "Doctor Bickers, I appreciate your concern for me and my practice..." She let that hang there for a moment, an unspoken accusation. Then she smiled. "My patients won't desert me. We've worked hard to create a friendly and *caring* atmosphere. They know I have their pets' best interests at heart."

Her message was clear. Bickers was a good vet as far as medical expertise, but he was horrible to his patients and their pets.

Bickers shook his head.

"And, just for the record, it was Blaise's idea to do the annex and I think it's a brilliant one. I hope for the sake of your patients you'll join in. Have a great day."

Her dismissal made his fleshy lips twist with anger. He stared hard at her for a long moment and then nodded, throwing her a mean smile. "We'll see if you can survive this. But just so you know, my offer was more than generous. When you come crawling back it will be considerably less."

Blaise opened the door for him and stood aside as he headed stiffly for it. He stopped in front of her and looked into her eyes. "You'd make a damn fine office manager, Ms. Runa. If you ever get tired of working for this foolish woman, I'll pay you twice what she can afford. Especially when all her clients leave her for me."

The bell on the front door jangled and Blaise gave him a smile she figured didn't come close to reaching her eyes. "I'd love to stay and chat, Doctor Bickers, but it sounds like our first client's here. Time to get to work."

As Blaise closed the office door behind him, leaning against it with an angry sigh, Mandy carefully placed Ivy on the floor and then gave a short, sharp scream. "What an evil troll he is."

"I'm thinking that might be an insult to trolls." Blaise walked over and dropped into Mandy's client chair. "He's wrong, you know. Your patients won't desert you. They know the difference between a great vet and an adequate one."

She shrugged. "I'm sure Adam and Jenny told you about the cancellations? He's not wrong about people's reaction to...things."

"I have a feeling it's all going to work out." The bell on the front door rang again and then, a moment later, one more time.

Mandy narrowed her gaze on Blaise. "What did you do?"

Blaise shrugged, her lips twitching.

"You paid people to come in today, didn't you?" Mandy was smiling, clearly joking. But when Blaise caught her eye, she paled. "You didn't?"

"Not exactly. I just told Jenny and Adam to offer them the office visit free. Of course, they'll still pay for your time and any meds or tests…"

Mandy stared at her for a long moment and worry started to gnaw at Blaise. Had she overstepped?

"Oh my gosh…"

"I'm sorry, if I…"

"You're a flippin' genius." Tears flooding her eyes, Mandy stood up and came around her desk, wrapping Blaise in a teary hug. "Thank you for being my friend and employee. I'm blessed to have you."

Something warm and gooey expanded in the vicinity of Blaise's heart and she felt her eyes tearing up too. "You're welcome. But I'm lucky to be here. I appreciate you letting me hang around while I figure out what I'm good at."

"You're exceptionally good at this, my friend." Mandy sat on the edge of her desk, her gaze fixed on Blaise. "I probably can't offer you the same salary as Doctor Bickers but, if you can do with a bit less in salary, I could give you some great perks in free pet care."

Blaise was touched beyond words. "You're offering me Alicia's job?"

"I am. Think about it. I could interview a thousand people and never come up with someone better suited to the job. Or someone I like as much."

"I *will* think about it. Thank you. I'm touched."

Mandy nodded. "Now, did you say something about donuts? I'm suddenly feeling ravenous."

7

*D*olfe picked her up at five and Blaise slid gratefully into the front seat. Ivy immediately jumped into the back to tangle with her brother and happy yipping ensued.

"You okay, honey? You look beat." Dolfe's welcoming smile turned into a look of concern. "No more problems, I hope?"

"No problems. It was just a really busy day." She dropped her head back on the seat and scanned him a look. "Dini's concoctions were a big hit. And Godric was able to clear most of Mandy's drug stash so at least we won't have to worry about that."

"That's great." He reached out and rubbed her shoulder. "Home, James?"

"If the route home includes *Panda Dragon*."

"You read my mind." He backed out of the parking slot and headed toward the street.

As they drove past the groomery, Blaise's gaze slid toward the spot where the black car had been. There was a big greasy-looking spot on the concrete where it had been sitting. "Is that oil?"

Dolfe glanced over and slowed. "Yep. Somebody needs a tune-up."

"That's where the car was the other morning. When I found Alicia."

He eyed the building thoughtfully. Finally, he said. "I got us an appointment with Representative Carter tomorrow. He's in town for his daughter's birthday."

"Good. What time?"

"The only time he could see us was three in the afternoon. Can you leave work?"

"I'd like to be there. I'll check with Mandy and make sure she's okay with it." Blaise smiled, remembering her big news. "She offered me Alicia's job today."

He eased the big truck into the flow of traffic. "Really? That's great. Are you going to take it?"

"I'm not sure."

"I thought you loved working there."

"I do. And it's fun being able to bring Ivy to work with me..." She chewed the inside of her lip thoughtfully. "I'm giving it some serious thought."

He reached over and clasped her hand, giving it a squeeze. "You know I'll support you either way."

"It's not much money."

"That isn't important. We're doing okay. We don't need to get rich." He grinned.

"That's good because if I worked there we certainly wouldn't get rich." She thought about her previous jobs, one as a bartender/waitress and one as a proposal manager. The two jobs couldn't have been more different, but she'd gotten something important from each of them. Still, she hadn't been ready to settle for either. And she wasn't sure she was ready to settle for the job she'd just been offered. "I'm really flattered she asked."

"You work hard and you've done a lot of good there. She'd be stupid not to ask you. And one thing I know about Amanda Willis is that she's not stupid."

Blaise nodded, feeling pleased by his support. "Did Brita get us the information on Josh Fawcett?"

"She did. He's actually staying at a senior and singles residence not far from here. In Silver City."

"We should go there tonight. I keep thinking that he's the most obvious choice for our villain."

"Are you sure? You look really tired."

"I'll get a second wind after dinner."

Dolfe hit the turn signal. "Okay, but if we're eating out we need to take the monsters home. It's too hot for them to stay in the car."

Silver Hills Senior and Singles Residence was a pretty place, three stories of light gray brick with balconies jutting from its front façade at regular intervals. Fragrant burgundy colored roses climbed the brick on one end of the big building. Enormous pots of flowers lined the portico leading to the front doors.

Blaise looked appreciatively around the place, enjoying the carefully nurtured grounds that were bright and happy with color. "Nice place."

Dolfe nodded, his hand on the small of her back as they headed toward the entrance. The double glass front doors experienced nearly constant traffic. People were coming and going, chatting enthusiastically.

A pretty, dark-haired woman with beautiful green eyes preceded them into the building, holding the door for them. Her smile was wide and welcoming. "Hello." She offered them her hand. "I'm Tricia Colombo, the Activities Director at Silver Hills. You're new. Are you here to look at the open apartment?"

Blaise and Dolfe shared a quick look. "Um, no," Blaise finally stuttered out. "We need to speak to Josh Fawcett."

The young woman nodded, her high ponytail dancing jauntily. "Josh. Yes." She frowned. "He's been getting sicker, hasn't he? He stopped coming to my activities." She pushed sadness aside and gave them a gentle smile. "Are you family?"

"No," Dolfe said. He handed Ms. Colombo his card. "I'm here on behalf of the Indianapolis Police. We need to ask Mr. Fawcett a couple of questions."

"Oh. Okay." She pointed toward a door marked, 'Office'. "The night manager's name is Vlad Newsome. He can give you Josh's apartment number."

"Thank you," Blaise told the other woman. She received a bright smile in response. "Any time. I hope you'll come back again."

"TC!"

They all turned to find a very large woman with a graying brown pageboy hurrying toward them. The woman clutched a fat orange striped cat in her arms and looked slightly panicked.

Ms. Colombo turned to Dolfe and Blaise and gave a nervous laugh before addressing the newcomer. "What's wrong, Agnes?"

The heavyset woman slid to a stop and skimmed Blaise a quick look, her gaze lingering slightly longer on Dolfe. "Mrs. Peoples is going to complain to Vlad about Tolstoy again."

Tricia seemed to be biting back a sigh. "What'd he do this time?"

Agnes frowned. "Why do you assume my cat did anything? That woman's just plain cranky. She taunts him."

"How exactly is she taunting him? He jumps up on the table and steals her food."

"She deliberately puts her plate close to the edge to entice him."

Blaise cleared her throat to stop a surprised giggle from escaping.

Tricia sent her a suspicious look, but her green eyes were sparkling. "I'm sure it will be fine."

Agnes expelled a frustrated breath. "You know Vlad would love to throw us out. She'll give him just the excuse he needs."

Dolfe cleared his throat and both women jerked a gaze in his direction, seeming to have just remembered he was there. "Thanks for your help, Ms. Colombo. We'll just go talk to the manager now."

A strident voice rose across the lobby, and an ancient woman shook a gnarly hand in Agnes' direction. "That varmint's stolen from me for the last time. He's literally starving me to death. Look at me. And then look at him!"

Standing next to her near the stairs, a petite and pretty elderly woman stood staring at Agnes, wringing her hands as everyone in the lobby did just as they were instructed. All eyes slid from the bird-like woman to the enormous cat in Agnes' arms.

No words were necessary.

"You eat like a pterodactyl, old woman. Nobody's starving you. And you need to quit throwing food at my poor cat. Tolstoy's getting fat. Tell her, Flo."

Flo, who was apparently the petite woman speaking to the pterodactyl, seemed to deflate. She finally shrugged and lifted her hands in surrender.

Tolstoy growled softly.

Agnes shook her head. "Sorry for the drama," she told Dolfe and Blaise. "If you're thinking about moving in don't let this..." she waved a hand back and forth between her and the conclave near the stairs, "--stop you. This is a really fun place to live."

Blaise stopped trying to hold back her grin. When she glanced at Dolfe, he was smiling too. "We're not," he told Agnes. "We just came to speak to Josh Fawcett."

Agnes' eyes went wide and she slid a guilty look toward the Activities Director. "Oh, um. He's in 304."

TC narrowed her gaze on the older woman. "And just how would you know that?"

"He lives down the hall from me. I spoke to him this morning..." She lowered her voice so much Blaise could barely hear her. "When I went to fetch Tolstoy."

TC's eyes went wide and she paled. "Tolstoy paid him a visit this morning?"

Gasps went up all around them. People backed away as if they'd seen a ghost.

Blaise felt like she needed popcorn. She was enjoying the show so much. "Is that bad?"

Agnes blew a raspberry. "Of course not. He's just very social."

"I'd better go call Doctor Bambast." TC turned to Blaise and Dolfe. "Please excuse me."

They watched the slender young woman hurry off toward the back of the lobby.

"My cat is *not* the Grim Reaper!" Agnes called after her.

The burst of laughter escaped before Blaise could stop it. Dolfe grabbed her arm and tugged her into motion. "It was nice to meet you," he murmured to Agnes before dragging Blaise, still laughing, toward the elevators.

"Grim Reaper?" Blaise said as the elevator doors slid closed.

Dolfe hit the button for the third floor and shook his head. "This is an interesting place."

"I like it," Blaise said. "I almost wish we could take that open apartment."

He lifted a dense, gold eyebrow. "I don't know about that, but it seems like Badly might fit right in here."

"He'd definitely give Tolstoy the Grim Reaper a run for his money," she agreed, laughing.

Josh Fawcett's door was open. Dolfe had grabbed his gun, pushing Blaise gently behind him with his other hand as he entered the dimly lit apartment.

"Dolfe..."

He waved his hand to silence her.

Blaise rolled her eyes. "Honeybun..."

Ignoring her, Dolfe hit the first door and spun across it, peering into the room with his gun focused inside.

A breathy gasp met his maneuver.

Blaise moved into the doorway and looked at the white-faced man sitting up in his bed with his arms lifted in surrender. He clutched a piece of whole wheat toast in one hand. "Take whatever you want. I don't have much, but you're welcome to all of it. Just don't shoot me."

Blaise put a hand on Dolfe's arm, gently pressing it down. "I tried to tell you. It's pretty common in these residences for people to keep their doors open. It encourages visitors."

Dolfe looked appropriately sheepish. He gave the man an apologetic smile as he slipped his Glock into the holster nestled in the small of his back. "Joshua Fawcett?"

The man swallowed hard, his hands...and the toast...still in the air. "Yes. Are you here to kill me?" He frowned. "Did my brother order a hit man so he could take the insurance?"

Dolfe blinked, clearly surprised. "If he did, I'm not the guy he hired."

Dolfe and Blaise shared a look.

"Do you think your brother would do that?" Blaise asked.

"Not really," Josh responded. He shrugged as if she'd asked him whether he liked chocolate pudding. "But he often jokes about putting me out of my misery." Fawcett frowned. "I *think* he's joking." He sighed. "Can I put my arms down now? I'm not very strong."

Blaise gave Dolfe a look. "Of course. We're so sorry to have startled you. In Dolfe's line of work an open door usually means trouble."

"What line of work is that?" Josh Fawcett asked as he placed his toast onto the plate in his lap.

Dolfe flashed his PI license. "Private Investigations. I'm a consultant with the Indianapolis police."

It was Fawcett's turn to look surprised. "Indianapolis? Why would they send you down here?" He turned gray. "Is Peter all right?"

"Your brother's fine," Blaise assured him. She sat down in a chair close to his bed. "Did you hear about what happened to Alicia?"

"His girlfriend," Fawcett nodded. "Yes. He called me. He was really upset. I only met the woman once but she seemed very nice."

"She was," Blaise agreed. "I actually worked with her."

"I'm sorry," Josh said. "But what does her death have to do with me?"

"The police suspect she might have been

murdered by a group called the *Medical Restitution League*. Have you heard of them?" Dolfe asked.

Fawcett hesitated a beat too long, his gaze sliding guiltily away from Dolfe. "No. I haven't. Who are they?"

Dolfe let silence pulse between them for a long moment. Blaise spent the time looking around the man's bedroom so she wouldn't get drawn into the trap. Dolfe liked to use silence as a weapon during interviews. Blaise hated awkward silences. And that usually got her in trouble.

The room was clearly more of a sickroom than a bedroom. Bottles of pills decorated every surface and the bedside table held a pitcher of water and a glass, along with an empty syringe and some discarded latex gloves.

"Have you asked Peter about them?" Fawcett finally asked.

Dolfe lifted a dark gold eyebrow. "Why would I ask your brother? Do you have reason to believe he knows them?"

Fawcett turned another shade lighter. "He might have mentioned a radical group to me."

Dolfe lifted the other brow.

Fawcett sighed. "Look, I don't know them by name. But Peter and I have talked about the need for groups like that one. People's priorities need to be changed. We don't condone murder, of course. But somebody's got to get this stupidity under control.

Do you know how much people spend on their pets every year? Thousands, in some cases. Not to mention the Federal resources given over to animals and animal care. And what about all the veterinarians? What if those young minds could be put to use helping relieve human suffering?" He shook his head.

"What you're suggesting is extreme," Blaise told him. "People love their pets. We love animals in general. That's not a bad thing. Kindness and compassion shouldn't be reserved only for one species. Our values as a society are reflected in how we treat all helpless creatures."

Fawcett sighed. "I know you're right. I'm just getting...desperate. Between the FDA, the state of health insurance today and the cost of medicines, so many people can't get the drugs they need. It's ridiculous."

"Is there a drug you can't get, Mr. Fawcett?" Dolfe asked quietly.

Fawcett moved the small plate holding his now cold toast around on his lap, refusing to meet Dolfe's gaze.

"Mr. Fawcett?"

His head finally came up. "I didn't kill that poor woman, Mr. Honeybun. Peter didn't kill her either. I couldn't tell you if she was mixed up with the... Medical...whatever group or if they killed her." His eyes filled with tears. "I just want to live. I'd give anything to find a medicine that would take this rot from my body."

"Anything?" Dolfe asked, his voice barely rising above a whisper.

Fawcett inhaled sharply, blinking tears away. "*Anything*, Mr. Honeybun. But I just don't see how killing Alicia would have helped me live even a single day longer."

8

*K*elly Carter looked even younger in person than he did in his campaign commercials. The thirty-eight-year-old, first-term congressman was still new enough at the game to be honest in his efforts and earnest enough to want to please his constituents. Grabbing hold of a bill as big as the *Shot at Life Act* was a bold move for a junior congressman, but Kelly Carter wasn't your average wet behind the ears politician.

He walked into the small diner while shaking rain off his small black umbrella, and looked around with a welcoming gaze and a ready smile. He was immediately surrounded by eager constituents and he didn't try to brush them off. Carter shook a few hands, asked people how they were doing, and actually appeared to listen to their responses.

The slender, dark-haired man who'd accompanied the congressman into the diner walked over and smiled at them, the smile too smooth to be genuine. He offered Dolfe his hand. "I'm Congressman Carter's assistant, Ted Smith. I apologize for the delay." He shook Blaise's hand. "The Congressman believes he should always be available to his constituents when he's out and about. He'll be with you shortly."

Dolfe made the appropriate noises. The other man turned away, standing beside the booth where Carter would sit with his hands crossed in front of him. He didn't speak again until the congressman joined them fifteen minutes later. Then he simply inclined his head when Carter dismissed him and went to sit at the counter.

The waitress skimmed an appreciative gaze over the politician as he slid into the booth opposite from Dolfe and Blaze. "What can I bring you, Congressman? Maybe a slice of peach pie with cinnamon ice cream?"

Carter grinned widely, his expressive hazel eyes sparkling with humor. "Just coffee, Madeline. Thank you." He rubbed his flat belly underneath a baby blue Polo shirt. "Living in Washington's doing a number on my waistline."

She grinned back, clearly charmed. "Stop fishing for compliments, now. You already know you're prettier than my mama's dahlias and smoother than a shot of whiskey on a cold Winter night."

Carter laughed deeply, his eyes crinkling as proof he did it often. "That was downright poetic, Madeline. Any chance you'd like a job as my speech-writer? I don't think the guy currently in the job even likes me. It's hard for him to make me sound good."

She snorted out a laugh. "I doubt that's true." She finally glanced at Dolfe and Blaise. "Can I get you folks anything else? Some more coffee, maybe?"

"Sure," Blaise agreed. "Thank you."

"Nothing for me, thanks," Dolfe said.

As she swayed in the direction of the kitchen, Congressman Carter reached toward Dolfe, shaking his hand in a firm, decisive grip. "Thanks for meeting me here. It's kind of a favorite haunt of mine. And it's close to home, so I can get back to my baby girl's party."

"How old is she?" Blaise asked.

"She's six today." He shook his head. "I still can't believe it. She seems to grow inches and years every time I go to Washington."

"That must be hard," she said, meaning it.

"It is. But the work is important. I'm honored to be doing it."

Dolfe couldn't help feeling like the man was spouting campaign slogans...stuff he'd said a thousand times in a hundred different diners just like the one where they were sitting. "Thanks for making some time for us. We won't keep you. I just had a couple of questions about the *Medical Restitution League*."

Carter shook his head. "No worries. Your daddy's been very kind to me since I arrived on Capitol Hill. I appreciate his support and I'm happy to repay it any small way I can."

"I wanted to thank you for the *Shot at Life Act*. It's huge and will hopefully save a lot of lives."

Carter nodded enthusiastically. "I agree, Mr. Honeybun. I'm very hopeful it will open up a whole lot of opportunities for people who'd otherwise get lost in the cracks." He leaned back as Madeline slid a steaming cup of coffee in front of him and placed the bill for their lunch on the table. "Thanks for comin' in, folks. Come on back. Any friend of the Congress-man's is a friend of ours here at *Hattie's*."

"We'll do that, thanks," Blaise answered with a smile.

When she'd walked away again, Dolfe leaned forward, lowering his voice. "Congressman Carter, can you tell me your motivation for the bill?"

"Please, call me Kelly. And if you're wondering whether I'm a member of MRL, I'm not. Naturally, we share some of the same opinions, but I don't endorse their methods. In fact, I think they're harmful to my cause. Their brand of activism is turning more people away than it attracts, I'm afraid. They believe people should be frightened and shamed into supporting a change in pharmaceutical law. I believe in the innate benevolence of the people of this country. I'll put my money on kindness over fear-mongering any day."

"How well do you know the members of the group?" Dolfe asked.

"Not well at all. I only know what I've seen on the news reports. Except for one person. The leader, David Byers. He actually contacted me when I first proposed the bill. We had a very civil conversation and I asked Mr. Byers to step back and let me get my bill passed."

"And what was his reaction?" Blaise asked.

Kelly gave her a sad smile. "He respectfully declined. He told me that successful wars are fought on many fronts."

"MRL considers this war?" Dolfe asked, frowning.

"I'm afraid so. At least if their leader's opinion is any indication."

"Did Mr. Byers say anything that would imply an interest in violence?"

Kelly sipped from his coffee. His brow knitted thoughtfully. Settling the heavy, off-white mug to the table again, he licked his upper lip. "Violence? Not specifically, no. But his tone was very aggressive." He looked up. "Mr. Honeybun..."

"Dolfe. Please."

"Dolfe. Am I to assume that, given your questions, you think Byers and the MRL might be responsible for that poor woman's death at *Precious Pets*?"

"The police certainly think they are," Dolfe answered.

"But you don't?"

Dolfe ran a fingertip over the handle of his mug.

"I'm inclined to believe Byers is innocent, myself," Carter told him quietly.

"But you just said he was aggressive," Blaise said on a frown.

"Aggressive, yes. Like a bully. I know a lot about bullies, Ms. Runa." He laughed, but the sound wasn't a happy one. "I wore polo shirts and talked politics in fourth grade. I was different. Kids don't like other kids to be different. As a result, I spent a lot of my time dealing with bullies. One thing I learned about them was that they're like cockroaches. They scurry from the light. I just can't see David Byers doing something so public. Something so sure to bring the spotlight of police and media attention down on them."

Carter slid out of the booth. "I could be wrong, of course. But the other thing I've worn all my life, aside from Polo shirts..." He grinned, exuding charm. "Is an instinct for people's motivations. It's been one of my strong suits in politics. I'd be willing to bet my last year in Congress that David Byers is a bully. But not a killer."

Ted Smith handed them a card as the

Congressman began making his slow way out of the diner. "Congressman Carter wanted you to know he's available whenever you need him. That's my personal number scrawled across the back of the card. If you need anything...particularly help dealing with the media on anything that touches on the *Shot at Life Act*...please give us a call. I'll be glad to help."

In other words, Dolfe translated, *don't screw up the Congressman's bill by stepping on the wrong toes.*

D avid Byers wasn't an easy man to run to ground. He wasn't at his home and his boss at the painting company where he worked said he'd called in sick. At six o'clock, Dolfe and Blaise decided to drive past the apartment building where he lived one last time before heading home.

Byers' apartment was dark and nobody came to the door when Dolfe knocked, but a neighbor down the hall stuck his scruffy head out and gave them the once over. "You people from the press?"

Dolfe reached for his PI license and flashed it as he walked toward the neighbor. "Private Investigator. I'm looking for David Byers."

"You and about a hundred other people." The man opened the door all the way and stepped into the hall. He was probably five feet ten inches of mostly stringy muscles and copious amounts of ink stretched over bones, without a lot of flesh. His over-long hair was frizzy, sticking out from his head in a messy tangle, and he smelled like old cigarette smoke. His raspy voice and leathery skin spoke of many years embracing the outdoors and bad health habits.

Byers' neighbor crossed his sinewy arms over his chest and leaned back against the doorframe, eyeing Blaise with a hungry expression. "You a PI too?"

She lifted her chin. "I am when I need to be."

His smile was slow and lecherous, until Dolfe stepped forward, sucking all the air from the space between them. The man's smile faded from his face.

"Have you seen David Byers today?" Dolfe's question was delivered in a brusque tone, bordering on a growl.

The man shrugged. "Not today. But I don't snoop on my neighbors."

Dolfe leaned forward a fraction, one long arm shooting out to rest against the doorframe behind Byers' neighbor, blocking his escape. "Where is he?"

Blaise frowned, unsure why Dolfe was coming on so strong with the man. "Dolfe, maybe..."

The door behind the neighbor suddenly opened. A big man with a darkly tanned face, graying brown hair and a gray goatee on a broad chin stood looking out at them. He seemed very familiar to Blaise. "I'm David Byers. You can stop harassing my friend."

Blaise was speechless. She glanced at Dolfe, but his attention was fully focused on Byers. "We need to ask you some questions about Alicia Prince."

Something hostile swept through Byers' dark brown gaze. His jaw tightened. Finally, he gave them a slight nod and glanced at the other man. "I got this Willie. Go on inside."

The skinny neighbor scoured a hostile glance over Dolfe and turned away, disappearing inside his apartment and closing the door hard behind him.

"What makes you think I know anything about this Alicia chick?"

"For one thing, I know you were at *Precious Pets* the other day. With the MRL."

Blaise's memory kicked in. Byers had been the big guy who'd gotten in Dolfe's face. The man standing near the street watching as they left. Leaning against his...

Her pulse spiked. "It was *you* in the parking lot that morning. The morning I found Alicia."

He frowned. "I didn't kill that woman. I never even went inside the building."

"Why should we believe that?" Dolfe asked him.

Byers shrugged. "I don't suppose you have any reason to believe me, but it's true. I went back to look for my cell phone. I'd dropped it the day before when we were protesting at *Precious Pets*."

"Did you find it?" Blaise asked, watching him carefully.

He reached into the pocket of his well-worn jeans and pulled out a phone. "It was in the grass near the street. Where I'd parked my car."

"You never went into the building at all?" Dolfe asked.

"I couldn't have even if I'd wanted to. I don't have a key."

Blaise knew that was a weak argument. Even *she* knew how to pick a lock. Any schmoe with a computer could watch a video on how to do it. "What time did you show up?"

"As soon as it was light enough out to see. I had to get to work."

"Did you see anyone else there? Another car?"

"No. Not until *she* drove in." He pointed to Blaise.

"I don't believe you," Dolfe told the man. "It's too big of a coincidence that you were there when Alicia Prince was murdered."

Technically, Blaise knew they couldn't prove that. Time of death for Alicia was closer to midnight. If it was Byers, that meant he'd hung out in the building for several hours. She blinked as a possible explanation came to mind, lifting her gaze to his. "Mr. Byers, were you and Alicia having an affair?"

Byers paled, his mouth opening and his bottom lip twitching. His gaze slid away as he dug for a response. Finally, he scrubbed a big hand over his face and expelled air in a rush. "It wasn't like that. She and I would just hook up every once in a while. It wasn't romantic or anything."

"But she had a boyfriend," Blaise said. Suddenly the tousled bed in the clinic apartment upstairs made sense. "Did he know?"

Byers shrugged. "She didn't talk much about him. Not that I really wanted to know. She said he gave her nice things, but he wasn't emotionally there for her." Byers shrugged. "I'm not sure what she was looking for because, unless it was a quick romp in the hay, she certainly wasn't getting it from me either."

"Mr. Byers, you were seen leaving the clinic minutes before Alicia was found dead," Dolfe said. "If you didn't kill her, how do you explain that?"

Byers shrugged. "She was alive when I left her around ten pm. She was planning to stay the night."

"You left?" Blaise asked. "But you were still there when I came in."

"I wasn't lying about my phone. I did leave it there, just not where I said. It was in the lobby, where we..." He flushed. "Anyway, I parked over by that other building in case anybody was paying attention and walked over to the clinic. The back door was still unlocked..."

"You didn't think anything of that?" Dolfe asked, looking suspicious.

"I thought it was strange she didn't lock up after

me. But Alicia was kind of drunk when I left. We were both drunk. I figured she just forgot."

"You went to the lobby?" Blaise prompted.

"Yeah. I found my phone on the long, wooden bench there. You know the one that looks like it came from an old church?"

Blaise nodded, doing an internal grimace. If Alicia and Byers...spent some quality time on that bench...Blaise thought she'd never sit on it again. "Did you go upstairs? Or into the kennel area?"

"No. I figured she was asleep and didn't want to wake her up so I just grabbed my phone and left."

Since Byers was answering questions, Blaise decided to go for broke. "One of the techs at the clinic saw you fighting with Alicia the other day, out in the parking lot. What was that about?"

Byers looked at his boots, frowning. "She wanted me to give her information on MRL."

"What kind of information?"

"It doesn't matter. She had the wrong idea about us. We're just trying to make positive change."

"What kind of information?" Dolfe repeated in a voice that was more command than question.

Byers shook his head. "It's not my information to give. There are people much higher up the food chain who'd be mighty pissed if I talked."

"Is it possible Alicia's boyfriend showed up after you left her the night before?" Dolfe asked.

"You'll need to ask him that. I don't know. I do

know that she was planning to call him, to tell him she was staying over. He was her ride since her car was in the shop."

Blaise and Dolfe shared a look. Peter Fawcett hadn't mentioned that phone call or any of the rest of it. He hadn't told them Alicia was staying at the clinic. Or that she would have had to keep him apprised of her timing and plans since he was her only ride.

And since he hadn't, Blaise had to wonder why.

"If you have nothing to hide, Mr. Byer," Dolfe asked, "why'd you park over by the grooming building?"

"I said I didn't kill Alicia. I didn't say I had nothing to hide. If any of the people at MRL knew I was sleeping with the enemy, there'd be hell to pay. Everything I've worked for would be lost."

9

*P*eter Fawcett looked surprised to see them again. In fact, Dolfe thought he saw more than surprise in the man's eyes. There might have been a tinge of fear there too. "Hello again, Mr...?"

"Honeybun," Dolfe provided.

"Do you have news about Alicia?" Fawcett looked from Dolfe to Blaise, clearly trying to determine how much they knew.

"Mr. Fawcett, can we come inside for a few minutes? We have a couple more questions for you."

Fawcett frowned. "I was actually just going out..."

"I think you should talk to us," Dolfe interrupted, his tone brusque. "Or we'll have to do this at the police station instead."

Fawcett swallowed hard and stepped back, indicating that they should come inside. Unlike the last time, though, he didn't invite them to sit. He stood in the entryway, his hands shoved in his pockets. The look in his eyes was slightly wild, like that of a trapped animal. Somewhere in another part of the house, the two little dogs they'd met in the previous visit were barking, the tone shrill and alarmed. "What's this about?"

"I think you know," Dolfe told him.

Silence throbbed around them as Dolfe waited out the other man. Guilt was a harsh taskmaster and it didn't hold up well under tense silence.

The hands in Fawcett's pockets moved, filling the quiet with the sound of jingling keys. Fawcett shifted from one foot to the other, cleared his throat, and then expelled a breath. "Okay, I admit I went to the clinic that night. But I swear she was alive when I left."

"Did Alicia call you to pick her up?"

"No. I expected her to. But when I didn't hear anything I called *her*. She sounded strange."

"Strange, how?" Blaise asked.

"I don't know, agitated might be the best word for it. She was breathing kind of fast and she seemed impatient to get off the phone."

Dolfe didn't need to look at Blaise to know what she was thinking. He was thinking the same thing. If Byers had been there...

"Did she say why she was agitated?" he asked the other man.

"She said they'd had a late emergency at the clinic. A dog that had just had surgery, and she wanted to spend the night there so she could keep an eye on it."

"But you went over there anyway?" Blaise frowned.

"Yes. I did. It was stupid. But I thought I'd surprise her. I brought her carrot cake from our favorite restaurant and a bottle of wine." Fawcett looked like he wanted to cry. "She wasn't happy to see me."

"She asked you to leave?" Dolfe asked.

He nodded. "Yes. But I'd seen the strange car in the lot. And she was flushed..." He swallowed hard.

"She wasn't alone?" Blaise asked gently.

Fawcett shook his head.

"What did you do?" Blaise asked.

His head came up and his eyes widened. "I left. What else could I do? I told her it was over between us and left." Fawcett shook his head. "I was really mad, Mr. Honeybun. I won't deny that. But I would have never killed Alicia. I..." He took a deep, shuddering breath. "I loved her so much."

"What time were you there, Mr. Fawcett?"

"Around ten o'clock, I think. I left here around nine thirty and had to stop for the dessert. I would have gotten to the clinic just after ten."

"Can you describe the car that was in the lot?"

"Dark, with sleek lines but kind of plain, like one of those foreign cars."

"Like a BMW?"

Fawcett frowned. "Could have been, yes. I do know it had a terrible oil leak."

"Thank you, Mr. Fawcett," Dolfe said. "Don't leave town. Detective Muldane from the IMPD will likely want to speak to you."

The other man nodded, looking miserable. If what he was telling them was true, he had every reason to be. In addition to losing Alicia forever, Fawcett had also inadvertently made himself a prime suspect for her murder.

"Mr. Honeybun, whoever she was there with that night, that's who killed her. You need to find out who he was."

If only it was that easy, Dolfe thought.

They said their goodbyes and headed for Dolfe's truck. "Let's get home. Ivy and Badly are probably crossing their legs about now."

Blaise nodded, unnaturally quiet.

Dolfe's phone rang as he climbed into the truck. It was Brita. "Hey, Brit. What's up?"

"Can you do me a big favor? Badgersville Police pulled Ralph Bickers in for questioning. Since you're already in the area, could you stop by and talk to him?"

Dolfe frowned, glancing toward Blaise. "The veterinarian? Why'd they pull him in?"

Brita sighed. "It seems one of his clients saw the report of the missing wolfhound on the news and she spotted the dog at Bickers' clinic."

Ralph Bickers wasn't nearly as snotty sitting in an Interview Room at the Badgersville Police Station. The ten by ten room was stuffy and unwelcoming, the walls consisting of concrete blocks painted an ugly green that were scarred and pocked from years of abuse.

Bickers turned a slightly haunted look on Blaise and Dolfe as they walked into the room, and then shifted his gaze to the tiny camera blinking from high in the corner, just beneath the drop ceiling.

Blaise scanned her gaze over that ceiling with a grimace. It was a disgusting Rorschach Test of multi-hued stains, the origin of which she didn't even want to guess.

"What is this, some kind of revenge tactic?"

Blaise returned her full attention to Bickers. The man was glaring her way, his fists clenched on the table top. He seemed to vibrate with an anger that was almost entirely focused on her. "Excuse me?" She frowned.

"You're protecting your friend, the ditz because I tried to buy her out. Is that what this is about?"

Blaise shook her head. The man was cray-cray. "I don't know what you're talking about..."

"I'm talking about you having me arrested on trumped-up charges. Did you come here so you could gloat?"

"Pipe down, Popeye," Dolfe said as he pulled a chair out for Blaise. "We had nothing to do with you getting arrested. You did that all on your own."

Blaise fought a grin as Dolfe neatly dispatched the petulant pooch snatcher.

"I did nothing. I have no idea why I'm here."

"Oh really?" Blaise couldn't resist asking. "I guess Agnes just walked into your clinic and locked herself up?"

The vet frowned. "Agnes? Who the hell is that?"

"The stolen wolfhound in your building."

The man blanched, his chins wobbling. "I...I found that dog on the street."

"Uh uh," Dolfe said. "You want to try again?"

"That dog was in a kennel at Doctor Amanda Willis' clinic," Blaise told him. "She was waiting to be picked up when she disappeared. Do you know where she disappeared from?" Blaise asked the nasty vet.

He just stared at her, his bulgy brown eyes filled with hate.

"Strange coincidence there," Dolfe said. "The dog was in the kennel we found Alicia Prince stuffed into. Do you have any idea how the dog got out of that kennel and into an enclosed area at the very back of your property?"

Bickers' chins wobbled another minute, and then he lifted his hands off the table. "This is all a horrible misunderstanding."

"Is it?" Blaise asked. "I'm not so sure about that. You see, the thing about dogs is they have no opposable thumbs." She lifted her hands and wiggled her thumbs in case he wasn't following. "They can't open kennel latches all by themselves. They need human type people to do it for them."

"Or opossums."

Blaise glanced at Dolfe, lifting her eyebrows.

"Opossums have opposable thumbs. They could open kennels too," Dolfe clarified. "And some frogs. The giant panda..."

Blaise fought the smile trying to curve her lips. "Thank you for that clarification."

"You're welcome," Dolfe said with a straight face.

"If you two are done being stupid..."

"Oh no," Blaise told him, grinning. "We're far from done with that."

"Absolutely true," Dolfe agreed. "I doubt you're done being stupid either, Doctor Bickers. For instance, I'm guessing you're going to try to go with the 'I found the dog on the street' defense despite how stupid it sounds. Have you run that one past your lawyer yet? Because I'm pretty sure he's going to recommend you try something else. Maybe an opossum walked into Doctor Willis' clinic and let Agnes out of her kennel. Maybe that same opossum scared Alicia Prince and she hid in the recently abandoned kennel and accidentally poisoned herself with a tube of ointment that had been inadvertently doctored..." He glanced at Blaise. "Which one of our critters with opposable thumbs could have doctored that ointment, honey?"

She tapped a finger on her chin. "Well, I guess we could go with a theory that the opossum had a best friend that was a frog or a panda, but that just seems silly. I'd say the opossum did it. He clearly had it out for Alicia..."

"Okay, okay. I get it." Bickers interrupted. He apparently couldn't take any more entertainment from his interrogators. "You don't believe me. But I'm not lying. When I was leaving Doctor Willis' clinic the other day I spotted the dog behind that old groomer's building. She was rummaging in the trash cans there. I recognized that she was valuable so I coaxed her into my car and brought her here."

"And it never occurred to you to bring her back to the clinic?" Blaise asked.

"I didn't know she'd come from there."

"It seemed like a safe bet that, since she was in the vicinity, Mandy Willis might have recognized her or known who her owners were. It would have been easy to check. You were right there."

"The dog's been on the news several times a day,"

Dolfe added. "Are you telling me you didn't recognize her? It's not like she's a Chihuahua or a Retriever."

Bickers shrugged. "It's not my job to save that ditz's butt. If she lost the dog, she deserves to get in trouble for it. Our clients trust us with their beloved pets..."

"Spare us," Dolfe snarled. "You don't give a rat's non-opposable thumbs about anybody's pets. You saw the report about the missing wolfhound and recognized an opportunity to make Doctor Willis look bad."

Bickers didn't confirm or deny. He simply held Dolfe's gaze.

"You're despicable," Blaise told the other man.

Bickers lifted a shaggy brow. "Does that mean you don't want the office manager's job I offered you?"

Blaise gritted her teeth so she wouldn't say anything she might regret.

She stood and Dolfe did the same. Blaise headed for the door, glad to be out of the tiny room that bore the stench of horrible person.

At the door, Dolfe turned back. "I'm going to recommend the Badgersville Police hold you for the full time allowed by law. I'm just not convinced you didn't steal that dog and kill Alicia Prince." He arched a brow when the other man began to bluster. "You might want to start praying that we don't find any evidence connecting you to the murder because we're going to be trying very hard to do just that."

B laise stretched her legs and sighed, letting the warmth of the evening sun ease some of the tension from her muscles. She sipped a smooth red wine and watched Ivy and Badly do happy zoomies around the yard. Blaise grinned as Ivy stopped short and her little brother ran right into her, his fat little form folding into a crumpled heap as she turned and looked down on him, her tail wagging.

Dolfe sipped his beer and flipped the steaks he was cooking on the grill. He hadn't said much on the way home from Badgersville. Blaise knew Bickers the nasty veterinarian had left marks on his soul. Dolfe didn't suffer fools who mistreated women, children or animals well. It was one of his finer qualities. But he'd get so angry he could barely contain himself. That was the reason for their playful banter in the interview room. The humor helped diffuse Dolfe's rage so he could do his job. He didn't like to lose control.

"That smells delicious."

Dolfe set his tongs down and closed the lid. "It does, doesn't it. I'm hungry." He walked over and slid into the lounge chair next to hers, grabbing her hand and kissing it. "How about you? Are you hungry?" Dolfe waggled his brows, making her laugh.

"Always. Have you met me?"

He leaned over and captured her lips in a tender kiss. When he broke the kiss he sat back, sighing. "What a day. Sometimes my job just sucks."

She nodded. "Everybody has secrets. Nobody tells the truth. And then there are those rogue opossums. They're incorrigible."

He chuckled.

Badly jumped on his sister, catching her off guard and flattening her, and then shot straight into the air as she yipped and tried to bite his ear. He hit the ground running, full speed, with ears streaming behind him, toward the patio, where he dove under Dolfe's chair without slowing. He skidded to a stop and smacked into the leg of Blaise's chair.

"Ouch! That must have hurt, little man." She reached down to try to scoop him up but he wasn't having it. The little terrorist nipped playfully at Blaise's finger and took off like a shot, doing another drive-by of his sister, who was trying to inspect a particularly interesting rock and didn't appreciate the black and tan whirlwind spinning around to distract her.

"They've been chasing lizards since we came out here," Blaise said as something skittered out from under the rock and scampered up the brick to the eaves. "When did we get so many lizards?"

"I'm guessing we've always had lizards. But we never set the lizard hunters on them before."

They shared a grin.

"Okay, let's try to sort things out, shall we?" Blaise suggested.

Dolfe swallowed beer and nodded. "We shall."

She sat forward, placing her wine on the small table next to her chair. "Our suspect list is long."

"Really long. Longer than my patience. Longer even than your ability to shop for shoes."

"Moving on..." she told him with a raised eyebrow. "First there's the boyfriend."

"Peter Fawcett. Upper middle class, by all accounts a decent enough person..."

"And a dog lover." Blaise marked a point on the air with her finger.

"Yeah. And admits he was there around the time Alicia was killed. He had a very good motive and acknowledges he left mad."

"Then there's the ex."

"Roger Jacks, a man who says he can't love his ex-wife but he can still like her." Dolfe frowned. "Or something like that."

"It's complex," Blaise said nodding.

"He wanted the dog enough to take her to court after the divorce."

"But did he want him enough to kill for him?"

"As motives go it's weak. But it's not out of the realm of possibility."

"Josh Fawcett," Blaise offered, picking up her wine.

"Angry and desperate. But too sick to leave his bed. I say we mark him off the list."

"Agreed. Then there's 'make me Ralph' Bickers," Blaise grimaced.

"A jerk. A Neanderthal. And an all-around ingrown hair. But I don't see him for a killer."

"Why not?" Blaise whined, causing him to smile.

"He'd pick on a defenseless animal but he wouldn't risk himself with someone who could fight back. Plus, there's no way Alicia would have let him into the clinic that night."

"All right." She pouted. "We'll take him off the list. But I'm keeping his name in my pocket so I can grab it quick if I need it."

"Deal." Dolfe frowned. "David Byers is another thing altogether. He's part of a group that's been known to be violent. He was worried about said group finding out he was sleeping with, as he put it, the enemy. What if he tried to walk away from the relationship...?"

Blaise's eyes went wide as the possibilities opened up before her. "And in a panic to keep him, Alicia threatened to expose him to MRL."

Nodding, Dolfe got to his feet and went back to the grill. He opened the lid and moved the sizzling steaks around until the fire flared again. "We have only his word that he left at ten o'clock. In fact, Peter Fawcett claims he was there a little after ten and there was evidence that Alicia wasn't alone."

"And he was certainly in a position to pull Agnes out of the kennel and shove her out the door. He wouldn't care what happened to her. The *Medical Restitution League* members are anti-animal."

"His car was definitely there when you arrived," Dolfe continued. "And MRL has a history of poisoning animals."

"He's got to be our guy," Blaise said.

"It certainly looks that way. I'll talk to Brit in the morning." Dolfe pulled the steaks off the grill and closed the lid. "These are done."

"Oh!" Blaise jumped from her chair, spilling a bit of her wine. "I forgot to finish the salad!"

10

*A*dam carried the rat bucket out of the storage room and set it in front of Odyssey's terrarium.

Blaise grimaced. "I wish you'd feed him when I'm not here, Adam. I hate watching it."

"Well, you're in luck then. Because we're out of rats. I've been trying to get to the supply house for days but with everything going on..." He shrugged his bony shoulders.

"I know. Don't stress it. Can't reptiles go a long time without eating?"

"Yeah, but that doesn't mean he won't be hungry."

Blaise skimmed a glance toward the cloudy glass of the huge cage. The snake was coiled on top of his favorite branch, his triangular head with the blunted snout pointed at Blaise. His eyes were reddish brown and unblinking as they fixed on her, the tongue dancing on the air as if he were licking his snakey lips. "He does look hungry."

Adam chuckled. "I think you're safe. But whatever you do, keep Ivy away from him."

Blaise shuddered with horror.

Hearing her name, Ivy popped her head up from the comfy little bed behind Blaise's desk. She yipped happily at Adam, earning herself a scratch under her tiny chin from the vet tech and some baby talk in a high-pitched, decidedly unmanly voice.

When Adam reached into his pocket and came up with a liver snack, Blaise felt she had to chide him a bit. "You're spoiling her rotten. Besides, Mandy doesn't want her to gain any more weight."

Adam straightened and winked at Blaise. "I won't tell if you don't."

Blaise shook her head, glancing at the door as the bell rang. A small woman with two leashes was pulled through the door by a pair of mastiffs. The dogs towed her across the room and flopped their big heads onto Blaise's desk, slopping drool all over the surface.

"I assume this is Dick and Jane for their annual checkups." Blaise scratched each of the friendly dogs in the wide space between their eyes. "They're adorable."

Their tiny victim...erm...owner scrubbed hair from her sweaty brow with a forearm, apologizing profusely. "I'm so sorry about your desk. They're not usually this naughty. Coming here gets them excited."

"They're fine. No worries," Blaise reassured her. She found their file and spun her chair around, sliding it into the appointment rack on the wall. "Have a seat and Jenny will be out in a few minutes to get their weight."

The young woman sighed. "Oh joy. The last time Jane kept slipping two legs off the scale so we couldn't get an accurate weight."

"Of course she did," Blaise said on a grin. "What lady wants the world to know how much she weighs."

The woman gave Blaise a slightly hysterical giggle and wrenched the big dogs away from the desk, only to be towed across the room to the dog toy basket.

Mandy came out of one of the exam rooms and saw the young woman sitting in the waiting room. "I'll be right with you, Paula."

"Okay. Thank you." The woman sucked air, looking like she'd be just as happy to sit for a spell.

Mandy looked at Blaise. "Could you come into my office for a minute?"

"Sure." She glanced at Adam. "Can you cover the front desk?"

"Happy to."

As Blaise followed Mandy back, Ivy bouncing

along with them, the doorbell rang again. The after-lunch crowd was pouring in. "I don't want to leave Adam by himself too long. The last time he got overwhelmed he offered Poor Mrs. Bickle a dog cookie and her schnauzer Jeff a chocolate bar."

Mandy snorted. "He should be fine." She closed the door and walked over to her desk. But she didn't sit down. Instead, she started pacing behind it.

Blaise could tell her friend was really upset. "What's the matter?"

Mandy glanced her way and then stopped, dropping to a seat on the front edge of her desk. "I got a call from Mrs. Ledbetter this morning. She wanted to let me know that Peaches had passed."

Blaise thought of the senior cat with one eye and an ear that was half torn away. Elderly Mrs. Ledbetter had coaxed the old alley cat into her home and the two of them had spent several years being each other's best friends. "Oh, that's so sad. I'm sure she's devastated."

"She is." Mandy wrung her hands a moment and then stood back up, pacing the narrow space in front of her desk.

"But that's not why you're so upset, is it?"

"No. It's not. Mrs. Ledbetter asked me to pick the cat up at her home this afternoon. She'd like her to be cremated."

Blaise was relieved. "I can do that if you'd like."

Mandy shook her head. "I'll do it. I want to tell her how sorry I am."

Blaise waited another moment for her friend to explain what was bothering her, but Mandy didn't seem able to focus on the real point of their conversation.

In the meantime, the outside doorbell just kept jangling. Blaise pointed toward the closed office door. "I should probably go..."

Mandy's head whipped up. "It's my fault Alicia was killed."

Blaise was stunned to temporary silence. For a moment she was unable to draw a breath. Had the woman she adored as a vet and a friend killed Alicia Prince? After a moment filled with tension, she finally asked. "Why do you say that?"

Mandy continued to wring her hands. "I..." She sighed, dropping her head into her hands. "Alicia and I fought that night. It was a horrible fight. She admitted that she'd been seeing Byers and that she was trying to get information from him about the group. Her plan was to get him to say something that would expose the more violent leanings of the group and then she was going to give the information to someone who could do something about it."

"Who?"

Mandy gave Blaise a confused look. "What?"

"Who was she going to give it to? Did she give you a name?"

"No. She refused. She said the fewer people she involved the better. I assumed she meant someone in the media."

Blaise frowned thoughtfully. It was good information. Between her, Dolfe and Brita they should be able to figure out who in the press Alicia had been talking to. But it didn't explain why Mandy thought she was responsible for Alicia's death. "Okay, so what did you fight about?"

"Alicia told me she was scared. Someone has been sending pictures to the clinic email. They were of our clients with giant red Xs over them. Alicia had been printing them off and deleting them before I could see them." Mandy leaned closer to Blaise. "They were pictures of client owners walking their pets out of *this* building, Blaise. This. Building."

"Okay, that's creepy..."

"One of them was Mrs. Ledbetter with Peaches."

The weight of Mandy's words hit Blaise like a sledgehammer. "Yikes."

Mandy nodded. "I made her give me the pictures. Agnes and her owners were also included. I was so relieved she was returned to them safely. Now I feel like I should warn everybody. But if I do..."

"Your practice will be done for sure," Blaise breathed.

"I know it sounds selfish. I shouldn't be worried about my own livelihood when people's beloved pets may be in grave danger..."

"But it's human nature. I understand." Blaise's mind was spinning. Then she realized Mandy still hadn't told her why she and Alicia fought. "So, what was the argument about, specifically?"

"I tried to get her to go to the police with what she knew and step back from it. I threatened to fire her if she didn't break up with Byers." Mandy sent Blaise an imploring look. "I didn't know what else to do. She was putting herself in such danger. Alicia loves..." Mandy sniffed, scrubbing a hand over cheeks that were suddenly wet with tears. "—loved her job so much."

"Did she agree to do it?"

"Yes. She did." Mandy fixed a horrified gaze on Blaise. "And I'm afraid that's why he killed her."

They were sitting at Brita's desk in the busy bullpen, activity and noise swirling around them. But the three of them were lost in their own fog, each respective face dark with horror. Brita knew only too well how the story would play out to the public.

Kill a human and people were sad for the loss, but threaten a cat or dog and people reacted with visceral objection and horror. It was a phenomenon that had once bothered Brita. She'd worried that people seemed to care more for animals than their own species. But then she'd become a fur mom for five rescued dogs. And one day it had hit her like a bolt of lightning why that was the case.

People saw pets like they saw children. Helpless and dependent.

Nothing spurred the protective instincts of your average American more than someone or something that was helpless to protect itself against the whims and unthinking violence of the worst among the population.

"After you called with the names, I checked. So far, from this list, only the cat and the wolfhound appear to have been affected."

"We don't know if the cat was tampered with," Dolfe pointed out reasonably.

"No. But we will," Blaise told him. "Mandy's doing an autopsy tonight. If Peaches was poisoned or harmed in any way, we'll know it."

"Hopefully these pictures are just meant to scare Mandy," Brita said, placing her hand on the photos spread across her desk. She recognized a couple of the pets and a few of the owners from her visits to the vet with her dogs. Her stomach twisted as she looked at them. A feeling that was much like having a family member threatened overcame her. "We can't let the media get this information."

Dolfe nodded. "You've run through the phone numbers Alicia called?"

"I've been over her cell phone with a fine-tooth

comb. There's nothing unexpected there. She called or texted her mother once a week and Fawcett a couple of times a day. She mostly texted Byers. She rarely called him."

"No other numbers?" Blaise asked, frowning.

"Nope."

"Does she have a landline?"

Brita glanced at Dolfe. "No. I even checked to see if there was a pay phone near her apartment or the clinic. Nothing."

Blaise's eyes went wide. "The clinic!"

Brita lifted a light brown eyebrow in question.

"Did you check the phone records at the clinic? She might have contacted the person from there."

Brita did a mental head slap. "You're right. She could have. I'll check that today."

"I'm just curious, what was the specific poison that killed Alicia?" Dolfe asked.

"Let me find the report." Brita rifled through the pile of papers she'd already gathered on the case. The intimidating number of documents from the open folder spilled across her desk, soon to be expanded even further by the addition of the photos Blaise had brought her. The lab report was near the bottom of the pile. "Here it is..." She scanned it quickly, frowning. "Aconitum."

"Like from the flower?" Blaise asked. She'd been designing flowerbeds at her and Dolfe's cozy little cottage. She'd admired the deep blue Monkshood flowers. They were beautiful, but the woman at the garden store had warned her away from them because of their dogs. "Those are really deadly."

"That's what I hear," Brita said, frowning. "Unfortunately, they're also pretty easy to come by so that doesn't help us find our killer."

"Anybody could have mashed up some seeds or petals and injected it into that tube," Dolfe agreed.

"Unfortunately, yes." Brita scrubbed her face with her hands. "What we need here folks, are a few more suspects to weed through."

Mandy came to Blaise at five pm to ask if she could stay another couple of hours. "Ralph Bickers being arrested has turned out to be a boon for our business. People who've been considering leaving him for years are apparently seeing it as a sign that the time is now." Mandy grinned. It was no secret that Doctor Bickers wasn't well liked...even among his clients...but he was a good enough vet many people had stuck with him anyway.

"Well, they and their pets will be better off for it," Blaise said.

"Undoubtedly true. But that leaves me with a problem tonight. Jenny has to leave early for a doctor's appointment and I have two emergency surgeries, so I need Adam. Can you man the desk for a little while longer tonight?"

"Of course. I'll just call Dolfe and tell him I'll be late."

"You're the best." Mandy gave Blaise an impulsive hug and then headed back to prepare for surgery.

Dolfe didn't answer his cell phone. She knew he was starting a new case that evening and would probably be out most of the night on a stakeout. So, she left him a message. "Hey, handsome. I wanted to let you know I'll be home late. I'm assuming you fed Badly and let him out for a potty break before you left tonight so all should be good. I'll feed Miss Ivy here. I'll see you when you get home. Love you!"

She turned to find Ivy lying in her favorite spot in front of Odyssey's terrarium, her little head on her paws and her soft, brown gaze locked on the enormous reptile. Odyssey was pressed against the front of his glass cage, his red-brown gaze fixed on the little dog.

Blaise shook her head. "Girlfriend, he isn't going to be your buddy. You need to stop posing your adorable self in front of him. He's looking at you like you're a TV dinner with fur."

Blaise briefly wondered if Adam had ever gotten a chance to buy more frozen rats for the big reptile.

She scooped her little dog up and kissed her between her big, round ears.

Ivy responded by swiping her tongue over Blaise's nose.

The exterior door jangled as Blaise was setting a bowl of kibble and one of water in front of Ivy. She looked up with a smile. Two clients she didn't recognize were coming through the door, faces flushed with worry.

Blaise settled down behind her computer and went to work. It looked like it was going to be a busy night.

She barely came up for air the next couple of hours. The sky was turning dark, the sun finally easing down behind a thick copse of trees on the horizon, when Blaise ushered the last client out the door and locked it behind her.

She looked around at the mess left behind by ten straight hours of chaos and sighed. She couldn't leave it the way it was. She set about straightening up, her mind sifting through the information they'd gathered and the people they'd talked to.

Something was bothering her. Some little detail that she'd missed tugged at her sub-conscious, leaving behind a trickle of unease.

As Blaise was straightening a painting of a multi-hued bulldog that the two mastiffs had nuzzled into crookedness that morning, it suddenly hit her. Her pulse jerked skyward.

"I'll see you tomorrow."

Blaise jumped and yelped softly, turning to

Mandy and laughing. "You startled me. I thought you'd already left."

Mandy smiled an apology. "I had to make a phone call to Purdue for a consult." She cocked her head. "Walk out with me?"

Thinking of the revelation she'd just had, Blaise shook her head. "I just have one more thing I need to do. I'll be right behind you."

"Okay, but don't stay longer than five minutes. You've had a long day too. You have to be twice as exhausted as I am."

"I won't."

"Promise?"

"Double pinky swear."

The two women shared a smile and then Mandy nodded, heading out the back way. A moment later, Blaise heard Mandy's car start up. She watched her friend drive out of the lot. Then Blaise went out the front doors and stood in the parking lot where she and Dolfe had been standing that day. The day they'd confronted the *Medical Restitution League* directly. The encounter had left her feeling unsettled for so many reasons. And she'd barely noticed what was going on around them at the time.

But she remembered the flash of reflected sunlight that hit her when she came through the door. Her gaze slid to the abandoned groomery and she pictured the big, black car that morning. Her mind swept past that memory, further back, to a man standing in the driveway...not far from where the big oil spot was now, holding up a cell phone as if he were taking video.

Blaise fought to pull the man's image into her mind. She thought he had a slight build and thinning dark hair. But he was partially obscured behind the phone and she couldn't quite pull his likeness forward.

Still. She thought she'd seen him somewhere before.

Then it hit her. And the memory nearly brought her to her knees.

11

*B*rita waited on the curb for Dolfe to climb out of his car. She'd decided at the last minute to call and ask him to join her when she spoke to Byers. He'd already interviewed the man so he had a baseline for their prime suspect's natural reactions.

She'd been all but ordered to bring Byers in on charges of murder, but she fully intended to get her own read on the suspect first.

Dolfe cocked his head as he joined her at the curb. "I'll admit I'm a little surprised you haven't already arrested him."

She sighed. "Don't tell me you think he's guilty too?"

"It seems too easy, doesn't it?" He shrugged. "I'm not completely sold. Neither is Blaise. But everything seems to point to him."

Brita turned toward Byers' apartment building. "That's what's bothering me."

Dolfe pulled the front door open for her. "I take it you're getting some pressure?"

"Only from everybody. The Sarge wanted to send uniforms over here this morning to arrest Byers. We've even gotten a call from Washington. People are scared. And now that word on the murder has gotten out..." She shook her head. "An MRL member was attacked this afternoon downtown and badly beaten. We need to tamp this down. An arrest would certainly help."

They took the steps to the second floor and slipped through the door into the hallway leading to Byers' place.

"Everybody wants this murder solved. And Washington wants the MRL removed from the public eye to give Carter's bill a shot at passing." She stopped in front of Byers' door and lifted her hand to knock.

The door was already open.

She slid Dolfe a look and pulled her Glock free of its holster.

Dolfe did the same.

Brita shoved the door open and skimmed left. Dolfe slid right, his gaze skating over the interior of the small apartment.

It didn't take them long to find him.

David Byers was sprawled across the kitchen floor, his eyes unfocused and glazed in death.

Blaise went back inside the clinic and dug out her purse. She prayed she still had the card Ted Smith had given them. She found it after several minutes of searching, turning her purse inside out and dumping all the contents onto her desk.

The business card was dented and torn, the Congressman's name nearly obscured by a coffee stain, but Blaise could read the number on the front. She dialed quickly, before she could change her mind, and got Kelly Carter's voicemail box. Fighting frustration, Blaise left a message.

She hung up and sat there for a moment, her mind spinning. Something told her she didn't have much time.

Blaise turned the card over and looked at the number there. Maybe Carter's assistant would know where he was. But, even if she found out where he was, she didn't know if the congressman would even see her.

Light flashed across the room from the television on the wall. It was set to the local news and, to her surprise, Congressman Carter's handsome face dominated the screen. He was standing in front of the police station, surrounded by reporters. His assistant stood just behind him, looking worried.

The camera panned away from Carter and showed a small group of protestors, holding home-made signs. Blaise recognized some of the faces from the *Medical Restitution League*.

She grabbed the remote and turned up the sound.

"...that's why we need to pass the *Shot at Life Act.*" Carter was saying. "Let's put all this violence and anger aside and come together. Obviously, human beings should have the right to take a chance on an experimental drug. We should be able to take that risk. It's our health...our lives at stake."

A cheer went up behind the Congressman. The camera panned once again to the protestors.

Blaise couldn't believe what she was seeing. When had Carter joined forces with the radicals? She glanced down at the business card again and made a sudden decision. Picking up her phone, Blaise quickly dialed the number on the back.

It rang behind her.

Blaise jerked around just as Ivy started to bark.

"I'd be willing to bet this is Aconitum poisoning again," Brita told Dolfe.

They watched the gurney wheeling Byers out the door to the waiting ambulance on the street.

"I guess we were right. Byers wasn't our guy," Dolfe told her.

She sighed. "Yeah. But we still don't know who our guy is, and the suspect list is longer than my dog food bill." Since Brita had five dogs that was pretty long.

The crime scene techs were currently dusting everything in the apartment for fingerprints. They'd recovered a paper cup that looked as if it had wine in it from the trash. If they were really lucky, they'd get either the prints or DNA of their murderer.

Dolfe snickered. "I'll call Blaise and tell her we're still looking for our killer."

"What the hell's goin' on?"

Dolfe looked toward the door, to the scruffy neighbor from down the hall. "Good timing. I was just about to come looking for you."

The man reared back as if struck, his mouth opening in shock. "Me? Why?"

Dolfe jerked his chin toward the scruffy neighbor. "Brit, this is Willie. He lives down the hall and was friends with the victim."

"Victim?" Willie's slightly jaundiced eyes grew wide. "What the...?"

"It's nice to meet you, Willie."

Willie forgot for a moment to be shocked and appalled when he got a good look at Brita. "It's *really* nice to meet you, sweetie. What's your name?"

She pulled out her badge. "Detective Muldane. I'll need you to answer a few questions for me, Willie."

The man crossed skinny arms over his narrow chest and glared down at her. "Am I under arrest?"

"For what? Did you kill your friend?"

Willie sucked air like a landed trout. "No way. You kidding me?" He slowly deflated as it sunk in. "Dave's dead? Oh no."

"When was the last time you spoke to him?" Dolfe asked the other man.

"Last night, I guess. We're both *Indy Eleven* fans. We watched the game together."

"Here?" Brita asked. "Or at your place?"

"We watched it here 'cause he has a better TV." Willie narrowed his eyes. "Why you askin' about last night?"

"Because your friend Dave was most likely killed between eleven PM and midnight."

Willie blinked several times in shock. He scrubbed a hand over his underwhelming chin. "I left around ten forty-five." He paled as he no doubt realized how close he'd come to a killer.

"Did anybody knock on David's door after you left?" Dolfe asked.

"You think I'd know that? I ain't nosy, man."

Dolfe's brows flew skyward. "Yeah, have you ever heard the name *Gladys Kravitz*, Willie?"

"No. Did she kill Dave?"

Brita twisted her lips against a grin. "You didn't hear any noise in the hall around that time?"

Willie shrugged. "No. But I wasn't here so I wouldn't."

"I thought you said you went home just before eleven," Dolfe asked.

"I left, but I didn't go home. I went to the bar down the street and played pool for a couple hours."

"Okay, then did you see anybody you didn't know when you were on your way out of the building? Somebody heading up to this floor, maybe?" Brita asked. It was a long shot but worth a try. The timing was close enough. He could have walked past the killer and not thought anything of it.

"There was the one guy."

Dolfe and Brita shared a look. "What guy?" Dolfe asked. "Describe him to us."

"There's not much ta describe. He was kind of average. Probably in his thirties. Good lookin' guy, I guess. Dressed all persnickety. You know what I mean?"

Dolfe did know what he meant. Or more precisely *who* he meant. He looked at Brita. "Call your boss. This is probably going to get ugly."

She watched him stride from the room, his cell

phone to his ear. "Dolfe, where are you going? Who are you calling?"

"Blaise. I need something she has. A phone number."

laise listened to her cell phone ring but didn't dare try to answer it. The man walking toward her from the darkened hallway held a gun and wore a cold smile that told her he wasn't too concerned about killing.

She was pretty sure he hadn't batted an eye over killing Alicia.

"Why?" She asked him.

He didn't even pretend not to know what she was asking. "She was going to mess everything up. Her boyfriend too. They were hatching a plan to go to the media with those pictures. I couldn't let them do that."

"They figured out it was *you* sending the pictures. You were trying to pin the blame for everything on the MRL." It wasn't a question. She'd finally placed the face she could only half see behind the cell phone across the lot.

"Publicity shots. Kelly had some bright idea to use them to help us sell the bill." He believed we could walk the line...grab support from both sides of the issue." Smith shook his head. "I realized the public wasn't going to support the bill unless they were angry or afraid of something. That's how you motivate today's voter. Haven't you heard the old media saying? If it bleeds it leads?"

Her phone started ringing again. Blaise glanced quickly down. It was Dolfe. Her finger itched to hit the *Answer* button. After a moment it stopped.

Blaise had to keep him talking. She needed to stall. "Why are you here? What do you want from me?"

"The perfect victim," he told her with a mean flash of teeth. "What do you suppose would happen if Senator Brick Honeybun's future daughter-in-law was killed by the MRL? Do you think Congress would finally act?"

"You're insane."

He shrugged. "Maybe. But I'm a man who knows what he wants and how to get it. If I can pull this off, my future in politics will be set."

Blaise's cell rang again. Her finger slid across the screen.

"I don't think you want to do that." In one, smooth move, Ted Smith scooped Ivy up and held her over Odyssey's cage.

Blaise's heart just about burst out of her chest. She jerked forward, against her will and cried out. "No!"

"Drop the phone."

She didn't even hesitate. Her expensive cell hit the floor with a crunch and slid under the desk.

Still, Smith held her little dog, wriggling happily in an attempt to get *into* the terrarium rather than away from the man who'd kill her if Blaise didn't do something fast. Ivy was a heartbeat away from death and all she wanted to do was make friends with the big snake.

Tears slipped down Blaise's cheeks as her heart broke. "Please put her down. I'll do whatever you want."

Smith pulled Ivy close and tucked her under his chin, scratching her tiny chest with the fingers of the hand holding her. The gun never wavered from Blaise's chest.

Ivy whined softly, looking at Blaise and giving her tail a half-hearted wag. She could sense Blaise's fear and wasn't sure what was causing it.

"She sure is a cute little thing," Smith said, lifting her so she could lick the tip of his nose. "It would be a shame to see her die."

Blaise's temper rose to fever pitch. She clenched her fists, helpless against the ice-cold monster holding her dog. "If you hurt her I swear I'll hunt you down and kill you myself."

"Good to know. I guess I'll have to dispose of you too."

A deep, deadly voice slid toward them from the

shadows. "Put the gun and the dog down and step away."

Dolfe!

Blaise allowed a brief surge of hope to fill her.

He emerged from the shadowed doorway behind Blaise and didn't look at her as he spoke. "Blaise, step back."

She shook her head, nearly blinded by her tears. "I can't. He's got Ivy."

"Honey, you need to step out of the line of fire." Dolfe stopped just inside the light, his gun trained on Smith. Despite the taut lines of fear turning his face into a terrifying mask, his hand didn't shake even a little bit. Blaise had no doubt he'd kill the other man.

Her only fear was that it wouldn't be in time to save her furry little monster.

"Blaise..."

"I can't, Dolfe. I'm sorry." She eased around, turning her back on Dolfe and addressing Smith. "I'll come to you and you'll put Ivy on the ground. You can use me to get out of here."

Smith's expression hadn't changed. He still looked arrogant and unconcerned. Blaise figured it was because he spent most of his time in the LaLa land of Washington DC, where no bad deed is punished and no one is held responsible for the trouble they cause. "I seem to have the advantage here, Mr. Honeybun. If you care about this woman at all, you'll put your gun down and kick it to me."

"Blaise..." Dolfe's deep voice held an element of fear, a pleading edge.

She sobbed softly. "I'm so sorry..."

Blaise took a step toward Smith.

His small mouth curved upward into a mean smile. The gun lifted an inch higher, silently threatening as Blaise eased closer.

"Honey, you need to trust me."

She stopped, her heart warring with her head. He was right. She'd always said she'd trust Dolfe Honeybun with her life. She actually *had* trusted him with it on a few occasions.

But could she risk Ivy's life on that trust? She closed her eyes and, as blades of pain shredded her heart, slid her hand behind her back and pointed toward the floor. A silent message for Dolfe.

Something must have given her away. Something in the softening of her shoulders must have warned Smith that he wasn't going to win.

In the blink of an eye, his arm shot out and Ivy was hovering over the terrarium again. Blaise didn't even have time to drop to her knees, out of the line of fire, before Dolfe had barked out an order and Ivy turned her head with a snarl and bit down hard on Smith's finger.

The man yelped in pain and opened his hand, Ivy dangling from his bleeding finger.

Dolfe fired and hit Smith in the shoulder. He jerked sideways, reeling backward from the pain, and hit his knees hard, the sound of bone cracking against tile a horrific echo through the room.

Blaise lifted her head as Dolfe reached her side, pulling her into his arms and burying his face in her hair. He didn't speak. He didn't have to. His heart was a frantic boom against her ear and his hands clutched her hips as if he would never let her go.

Blaise leaned into him, her heartbeat matching his. And let the comfort of being in his arms pull some of the terror from her bones.

Then her eyes shot open. "Ivy!"

Her gaze shot to the terrarium and frantically searched it.

Odyssey was slithering along the front glass surface, his tongue snapping out to taste the gunpowder flavoring the air.

And on the floor, in her usual spot watching the big reptile. Miss Ivy sat like a furry little statue, her adoring gaze on her hungry and reluctant friend.

12

"*H*ow?" she asked Dolfe later, clutching Ivy tight and watching Badly chase a horsefly around the patio with happy yips. The fly was in no danger of being caught or eaten. Instead, it seemed to be taunting the fat little dog, enjoying the game even more than Badly.

Dolfe watched the puppy play. His expression grim. "I still have nightmares about seeing that knife to her throat. After that, I decided I'd teach her some self-defense moves."

Blaise buried her nose in Ivy's fur and inhaled deeply, enjoying the little dog's sweet scent. "That was very effective. What was that you yelled at her?"

Ivy wriggled free and jumped down, running off to help her brother catch the fly.

"*Dårlig mand*," Dolfe said softly. "It means *bad man* in Danish. I knew a canine cop once who had a

Dutch German Shephard and that was his trigger word."

She scrunched up her face. "Why Danish?"

"Because it's unlikely she'll ever hear it on the street and react by mistake."

"Genius." She laid her head back and closed her eyes. "I'm glad I trusted you."

"There was a moment there when I wasn't sure you would." His tone was teasing, but Blaise heard the touch of hurt in it.

She looked at him, reaching for his hand and placing it against her heart. "I know. I'm sorry. I was just so scared."

"I was terrified. For both of you."

She nodded.

They sat in silence for a few minutes, just enjoying the quiet night and the antics of the dogs. But finally, curiosity got the best of her.

"You spoke to Brita?"

"While you were in the shower."

"And?"

He sighed, squeezing her hand in his big, warm grip. He held it while he told her an almost unbelievable story. A story filled with hate and fear and a lust for power that drove a man to do terrible things.

"Not that I really care but, is Smith all right?"

"He'll be fine. But he won't be picking fights in prison," Dolfe said with a grim smile. "At least not with that arm."

"Has he admitted to killing Alicia and Byers?"

"No. He's too smart for that. He lawyered up immediately. But the search of his place came up with a small bottle filled with Aconitum. The pictures he used to frighten Mandy are still in his cell phone. And Willie positively ID'd him as the man he passed on the way down from Byers' place. He's going to prison."

"Will Carter help him?"

"Not a chance. Carter wanted to work with MRL. He wanted all parties on board to help him pass the bill. He's already distancing himself from Smith."

"Good." She shook her head. "He'll have his hands full getting that bill passed," she said on a frown. "The opposition's already blaming his bill for the two murders and the radicals."

"Politics as usual," Dolfe said. He gave her hand a squeeze. "It will pass in the house. And Dad's gonna help him round up enough votes in the Senate."

"I hope so. That bill's been a long time coming."

Badly bounced over and jumped up on Blaise's chair, evading her hands when she tried to snuggle him close and attacking her big toe instead, licking and nipping at it as she squirmed and giggled.

Finally, Dolfe snagged the little man and placed him in her lap. The puppy licked her hand sweetly and then circled three times and collapsed, giving a tiny sigh before falling instantly asleep as only a puppy can do.

She smiled. "He's growing up so fast."

"He'll be starting self-defense lessons soon too."

She gave him an alarmed look. "Seriously? He's already a prickly little porcupine. Do we really want to teach him to bite on command?"

"It's the 'on command' part that's key."

She shook her head. "Why'd he do it?"

"Smith? Political aspirations. He wanted to be known as the man behind the man who got the bill pushed through. Unfortunately, Smith thinks ruthlessness is the most important personality trait in Washington."

"He could be right about that."

"My dad and Kelly Carter would seem to disprove it."

"You're right. So, he came to the clinic after Byers left that night?"

"Alicia called him. We found the call listed in the clinic phone records. Byers had seen Smith snapping pictures of clients. When the threatening photos started turning up, Alicia and Byers made the connection. Alicia confronted Smith and demanded he tell her what he was up to."

"And he killed her to keep her quiet about the pictures."

"Then when he found out her source for the information, he killed Byers to close the loop."

She frowned. "But how'd he find out?"

"After Alicia turned up dead, Byers tried to contact Carter to tell him his assistant might be the killer."

"But Smith got the voicemail, just like he intercepted mine."

"Yep."

"Oh what a tangled web we weave." She thought about it for a minute and then cocked her head. "Agnes and Peaches?"

"Smith set the wolfhound loose after dispatching Alicia, and Mandy's autopsy showed no signs of poisoning in Peaches. It looks like Smith was more about threatening the animals than actually hurting them."

"Unfortunately, he didn't seem to have the same compunction about killing people."

"True dat." Dolfe narrowed his gaze on her. "Have you decided if you're going to take Mandy's job offer?"

Blaise bit her lip. "I've really been struggling." She expelled a sad breath. "But I think I'm going to turn it down."

"I'm a little surprised."

"Yeah, to tell you the truth, so am I. I've loved working there. And I love Mandy. But it just doesn't feel right to me. I think my perfect job's still out there."

"Well, whatever that job is, you'll know it when

you find it."

"I think you're right." She smiled, feeling happy with her decision.

He tugged her hand. "Come on, let's get these little monsters inside. I have an appointment with their mommy for some 'us' time."

She let him pull her to her feet, cradling the comatose puppy in one arm. When Dolfe made as if to tug her toward the house, she resisted, leaning in for a kiss.

When she broke it a few minutes later, Dolfe grinned. "Not that I'm complaining but, what was that for?"

"For caring about these little guys as much as I do. And for doing whatever it takes to keep us all safe."

He dropped an arm around her shoulders and urged her toward the door, whistling for Ivy. "You know, these dogs are much easier to train than you are."

She grinned. "Yeah, but I'm worth it."

"Yes you are, future Mrs. Honeybun. You definitely are."

Thanks for reading **Toxic Tech**! Would you like to read more Blaise and Dolfe stories? As my gift to you, here's Chapter One of **Book 1: Homicidal Holiday!**

It was a simple holiday getaway...a chance to regroup and figure out how to move forward after losing the man of her dreams...then she witnessed a murder on the beach...

HOMICIDAL HOLIDAY

Dolfe Honeybun stood in the shadows and watched his ex-girlfriend flirt with a tall, annoyingly good looking guy on line at a popular nightclub. She looked spectacular as usual; her long, slimly curved form lovingly embraced in some kind of shimmery white material which didn't cover nearly enough of her.

He frowned as the man she was speaking to leaned forward, whispering something into Blaise's ear as his hand slipped over her hip and stopped on her firm, round behind. Dolfe's pressure spiked and he was moving forward before he could stop himself.

He crossed the street to the blare of horns, almost entirely oblivious to oncoming traffic. Red flares were flashing in front of his eyes and his hands were clenched into fists. As he plummeted heart first into complete loss of control, Dolfe took some comfort in the fact he hadn't pulled his gun.

It didn't matter that Blaise deftly, and with a smile, removed the man's hand from her butt. It didn't even matter that she walked away. Because the other guy's lust-saturated gaze followed her sexy sway down the sidewalk, her heels click-clacking rhythmically on the concrete as she walked.

Dolfe decided at that moment the man had to die.

He headed straight for the cocky, overdressed buffoon who was accepting knuckle bumps from his friends by way of celebrating that he'd copped a feel from the gorgeous black woman with the million dollar smile.

Dolfe would rip him into such small pieces his friend Brita Muldane, the cop, wouldn't even be able to find the body.

The weasel turned as Dolfe stormed toward him, his unintelligent blue eyes widening at the look on Dolfe's face. He took a step back as Dolfe reached for him.

Dolfe's ears roared. He could taste every beat of his heart as his pulse surged to the danger zone. And adrenaline had him by the throat as he grabbed pretty boy's expensive tweed coat by the lapels and dragged him off the ground.

"Hey!" the guy's friends coughed out. But when Dolfe turned his murderous gaze on them, they lifted their hands and stepped back. Apparently judging their friend to be unworthy of having their own blood spilled.

Somewhere on the edges of Dolfe's awareness a familiar click, clack, click, clack intruded, the sound speeding and getting louder as it got closer.

He shook the offensive pup like a rag doll and pressed his face close. The young punk stank of expensive cologne. He was darn lucky he didn't smell like Blaise.

That would have signed his death warrant for sure.

Click, clack, click, clack…

The guy tried tugging Dolfe's hands from his coat without any success. "What the hell, man?"

"You think that's the right way to treat a lady?" Dolfe growled into his face.

The guy blinked under every word, as if he were being pelted with buckshot. "What lady?"

Dolfe's growl deepened and the guy's heels lifted another inch from the ground. "Wrong response, punk."

Click, clack, click, clack…

"Hey come on, dude," the guy whined. "Blaise is just a friend."

"You always run your hands all over your friends' asses?" Chuckling from the guy's disloyal friends abruptly stopped as Dolfe skimmed them with a hostile, green glance. When they were properly quelled, Dolfe refocused his hostility where it belonged. "You want to feel up *my* behind?"

More chuckling.

Click, clack, click, clack...

The guy grimaced. "I don't play for that team, dude."

Dolfe shook him. "But I thought you always felt up your friends. I'm thinking you and me are friends."

"Darn it, Dolfe!" A soft, long-fingered hand gripped his arm, tugging on it. "Let him go."

Dolfe inhaled deeply, her exquisite scent spearing his senses and rolling like warm butter over his nerves. "Stay out of this, honey. The guy dissed you. I'm takin' care of it."

She tugged harder. "Dolfe Honeybun, you let go of him right now and come with me."

He finally turned to look at her and forgot to breathe. He'd almost forgotten how beautiful she was...how delicious she looked and smelled. He frowned, turning back to the punk. "Learn respect you little jerk." He dragged the guy off the ground another half inch just to drive home his point and then flung him away.

The punky kid stumbled backward several steps, his friends catching him before he landed on his ass.

Dolfe turned away and immediately forgot him. He grinned. "Hey, honey. You look stunning as always."

Blaise glared at him, her long, slender arms crossed over her chest. Her pretty brown eyes flashed with anger. "Let's take a little walk, shall we?" She started down the sidewalk, her four inch high spiked heels click-clacking angrily against the concrete.

Dolfe winked at the disgruntled punk and started after her, his gaze sliding over the crowd of males to ensure nobody else got any ideas about disrespecting his girl.

He blinked, his stomach twisting with disappointment. Scratch that. Blaise was now his ex-girlfriend. They'd broken up the week before. Primarily because of the very thing he'd just interrupted.

Blaise hit the corner and stopped, turning back to him with a decidedly unhappy look on her beautiful face. The golden light from the streetlamp illuminated her delightful form, making her look like an ebony-skinned angel with fire in her veins. She fairly vibrated with rage. Her whole frame was taut with it, her delicate jaw working over the words she no doubt wanted to fling his way.

She didn't even wait for him to reach her before she launched. "What is wrong with you? What are you doing stalking me?"

Dolfe drifted to a stop and shoved his hands into his pockets, holding her fiery gaze. He was fully aware he'd acted badly, but he didn't care. He'd do it again in a heartbeat.

She didn't seem to require a response from him anyway. She was too busy pelting him with her angry verbal assault. "We broke up, remember? We're no longer an item, you and I. We're finished, *kaput*, *finito*." She stepped closer, poking him in the chest with every word. "I don't answer to you anymore and if I want to flirt with another guy I'll do it all day long. *Capiche*?"

He lifted an eyebrow and crossed his arms, telling himself the tearing sensation in his chest cavity was just the aftermath of a bad lunch burrito. Unfortunately, he knew better.

She was flailing his heart into tiny little pieces. "I'm sorry, honey. But I'm not gonna just stand around and watch some punk manhandle you on the street."

She took a deep breath and expelled it, obviously striving for calm. "I had it handled, Dolfe."

He shook his head. "No, no you didn't. You sweetly removed his hand and smiled at him. Kneeing him in the crotch would be handling it. What you did was just short of a promise."

"Shut up, Honeybun."

He twisted his lips against a cocky response and glanced away, knowing she deserved better. She had a right to be mad. "I don't regret what I did."

"I'm sure you don't. That's the problem."

He covered the last of the distance between them and wrapped an arm around her tiny waist, pulling her close. She gasped in surprise and struggled against his grip. "No. The *problem* is that I can't stand the idea of you with another guy. The *problem* is that you should be in my bed right now, writhing and moaning underneath me." Her eyes glittered with unshed tears and he suddenly felt guilty for dragging them both through the mire again. Dolfe lowered his head so that her lush lips were close... too close. Close enough for him to feel the soft hitch in her breath that told him she wasn't nearly as disinterested as she pretended. "The *problem* is that you make me crazy and the longer we're together the crazier I get." Dolfe touched her lips in a soft, prolonged kiss and then forced himself to step back. "I wasn't stalking you." He scrubbed a hand over his chin because he needed to do something with it. If he didn't, he'd be grabbing her up again and he wasn't sure he'd be able to let her go a second time. "I'm working."

She frowned. "I'm supposed to believe you just happened to show up at the same club where I was?"

Dolfe turned away. "Believe it or not. I've been here for two hours, watching for the most likely cheating spouse of my client." He looked around. "I'll walk you to your car. Where did you park?"

She stepped past him. "I'm going back to the club."

Anger spiked and Dolfe gritted his teeth against it. She was right. They weren't together anymore. It sucked planet-sized lemons but it was the reality he'd have to get used to. After all, it had been his idea to split. He didn't respond as she walked away... didn't trust himself to speak. Instead, he followed along behind to make sure she got safely inside, the click, clack, click, clack of her heels pinging against his nerves like bullets. And doing just as much damage to his heart.

"Are you sure you're up for this?"

Blaise turned to the man sitting next to her, forcing a smile onto her face. "Of course. Why?"

Dugald Richards shrugged, his dark chocolate gaze sliding over her assessingly. "You don't seem very excited about our trip."

Blaise reached over and squeezed his arm. The bulging flesh was like iron under her fingers. It reminded her of Dolfe. She barely kept from sighing, biting her bottom lip instead. Everything reminded her of Dolfe. "I'm just a little tired." She *was* tired, in fact she'd been tired for two weeks, since Dolfe had told her he couldn't be with her anymore. She was starting to think it was depression. Which was why when her best friend since high school asked her if she wanted to come to Florida with him over Christmas she eagerly agreed.

Maybe some sun and partying would make her

feel better. The plane's engines roared as they prepared to land in Miami and the pilot came on the intercom to verify that they would be on the ground in ten minutes.

Still, the prospect of parties just didn't give her the jolt of excitement it used to. It was the constant partying that had come between her and Dolfe. He was a serious man. A man whose job as a private investigator meant he was always dealing with the seedier side of life. Dolfe knew intimately how dangerous the world could be. He lived it every day. He'd seemed fascinated by her carefree, party girl ways in the beginning. But after a few months, her almost manic need for fun and frivolity started to rub him the wrong way.

Blaise knew he had a point. She was careless at times. Unthinking. But she was young and beautiful and she wanted to enjoy it while she could.

Unfortunately, she wasn't enjoying it anymore.

Scrunched into the comparatively tiny Business Class seat, Dugald wrapped his long fingers around her hand and squeezed. "Reggie and the gang are meeting us at the hotel in an hour. We'll have dinner and drinks on the terrace and then go to a party they say is *the* big event of the season." He tried to stretch his long, long legs and grimaced as his knees bumped up against the seat in front of him.

Blaise dug for some enthusiasm and tried to focus it into her answering smile. "That sounds perfect. I want to walk on the beach every day while we're here. And eat seafood until it's coming out my ears."

Dugald laughed his baritone laugh. "None of that fishy stuff for me. I'm gonna eat Cuban food until my eyes turn the color of peppers."

The steward started down the aisle, collecting trash and telling people to close their trays in preparation for landing. Dugald adjusted his seat into the upright position as the steward lifted a sandy blond eyebrow at him. Her friend saluted and made the guy laugh. Blaise grinned. He was always making people smile. It was his best skill other than playing basketball, which he'd done professionally for six years until the Indiana Pacers had cut him from the roster the previous year.

Dugald had taken the change with his usual grace and good humor. He'd always wanted to open a restaurant, he told Blaise. So that was what he'd done.

Not surprisingly for anybody who knew him, *Dugald's* was on its way to becoming an Indianapolis favorite. Partly because it was a favorite spot for the Pacers players and management to hang out. And partly because of Dugald himself. Like Blaise, her friend loved people and he was good with them.

She'd been a little surprised when he'd asked her to come with him to Florida. The holiday season was a busy time in the restaurant. But Dugald had a good manager he trusted, and he said he needed a break.

Lord knew Blaise needed one too. She only hoped the time away would help her forget the way Dolfe's hands had felt on her body...or the decadent delights his sexy mouth performed on her.

Blaise's body tightened on the thought and her mood took a dip. She pushed the painful thoughts away. Dolfe no longer wanted to be with her. He'd moved on. And she was determined to move on too. She'd even formed a plan for how to do that, and her current trip might be just the thing she needed to put that plan into play, turning Dolfe Honeybun and their short but incendiary relationship into a distant memory. As Blaise left the 737 and stepped into the busy Miami terminal, taking Dugald's muscled ebony arm, the thought made her feel a little bit better.

Check out all the Gainfully Employed Mysteries: https://www.samcheever.com/series.html#gainfullye mployed

ALSO BY SAM CHEEVER

If you enjoyed Toxic Tech, you might also enjoy these other fun mystery series by Sam. To find out more, visit the **BOOKS** page at www.samcheever.com:

Gainfully Employed Mysteries

Honeybun Heat Series

Silver Hills Cozy Mysteries

Country Cousin Mysteries

Yesterday's Paranormal Mysteries

Reluctant Familiar Paranormal Mysteries

ABOUT THE AUTHOR

USA Today and *Wall Street Journal* Bestselling Author Sam Cheever writes mystery and suspense, creating stories that draw you in and keep you eagerly turning pages. Known for writing great characters, snappy dialogue, and unique and exhilarating stories, Sam is the award-winning author of 80+ books.

To learn more about Sam and her work, visit or contact her at one of the following online hotspots:
www.SamCheever.com
samcheever@samcheever.com